A Word from Stephanie about Being in Show Biz

When my school decided to have its own TV news program, I jumped at the chance to be producer. But before I could have the job, I had to convince everyone I could come up with fun, creative ideas for the show.

That's when the trouble started. I couldn't come up with anything new and different for *Scribe TV*—until I asked my friend Maura for help. She gave me some great ideas. And I told my friends all about them. Everyone thought Maura's ideas were awesome—but they also thought they were mine! And because of them, I was voted producer of *Scribe TV!*

Should I tell the truth, and risk my position as producer? Or keep lying and risk hurting Maura's feelings? I need some advice—and quick! Good thing there are plenty of people to ask for advice in my house.

In fact, right now there are nine people and a dog living in my house. And for all I know, someone new could move in at any time. There's me, my big sister, D.J., my little sister, Michelle, and my dad, Danny. But that's just the beginning. When my mom died, Dad needed help. So he asked his old college buddy, Joey Gladstone, and my uncle Jesse to come live with us, to help take care of me and my sisters.

Back then, Uncle Jesse didn't know much about

taking care of three little girls. He was more into rock 'n' roll. Joey didn't know anything about kids, either—but it sure was funny watching him learn!

Having Uncle Jesse and Joey around was like having three dads instead of one! But then something even better happened—Uncle Jesse fell in love. He married Rebecca Donaldson, Dad's co-host on his TV show, *Wake Up, San Francisco*. Aunt Becky's so nice—she's more like a big sister than an aunt.

Next Uncle Jesse and Aunt Becky had twin baby boys. Their names are Nicky and Alex, and they are adorable!

I love being part of a big family. Still, things can get pretty crazy when you live in such a full house!

FULL HOUSE™: Stephanie novels

Phone Call from a Flamingo
The Boy-Oh-Boy Next Door
Twin Troubles
Hip Hop Till You Drop
Here Comes the Brand-New Me
The Secret's Out
Daddy's Not-So-Little Girl
P.S. Friends Forever
Getting Even with the Flamingoes
The Dude of My Dreams
Back-to-School Cool
Picture Me Famous
Two-for-One Christmas Fun
The Big Fix-up Mix-up
Ten Ways to Wreck a Date
Wish Upon a VCR
Doubles or Nothing
Sugar and Spice Advice
Never Trust a Flamingo
The Truth About Boys
Crazy About the Future
My Secret Secret Admirer
Blue Ribbon Christmas
The Story on Older Boys
My Three Weeks as a Spy
No Business Like Show Business

Club Stephanie:

#1 Fun, Sun, and Flamingoes
#2 Fireworks and Flamingoes
#3 Flamingo Revenge

Available from MINSTREL Books

FULL HOUSE™
Stephanie

No Business Like Show Business

Gail Herman

A Parachute Book

READING

A MINSTREL® BOOK

Published by POCKET BOOKS
New York   London   Toronto   Sydney   Tokyo   Singapore

A MINSTREL PAPERBACK *Original*

A Minstrel Book published by
POCKET BOOKS, a division of Simon & Schuster Inc.
1230 Avenue of the Americas, New York, NY 10020

A PARACHUTE BOOK

READING Copyright © and ™ 1998 by Warner Bros.

FULL HOUSE, characters, names and all related indicia are trademarks of Warner Bros. © 1998.

ISBN: 0-671-01725-X

First Minstrel Books printing May 1998

10 9 8 7 6 5 4 3 2 1

A MINSTREL BOOK and colophon are registered trademarks of Simon & Schuster Inc.

Cover photo by Schultz Photography

Printed in the U.S.A.

CHAPTER
1

♦ ◄ ◗ ♦

Stephanie Tanner skimmed the titles in the book-store's TV section. She settled on the biggest, thickest book she could find and quickly read through the table of contents.

Yes! This was exactly the book she needed. Steph closed the book and went to find her good friends, Allie Taylor and Darcy Powell.

Darcy stood in the mystery section, holding a paperback in each hand. Darcy loved mysteries. She planned to read one a week as soon as school let out for the summer. Allie stood next to her, holding a teen romance novel.

Sometimes Stephanie thought Darcy and Allie were complete opposites. Even their choices in books were different.

Allie was small for an eighth-grader, with light

brown hair and green eyes. She was shy, level-headed, and not terribly athletic.

Darcy was tall and graceful with tightly curled black hair. She was outgoing, and a natural athlete who loved sports.

Stephanie and Allie had been best friends since kindergarten.

Darcy's family moved to San Francisco from Chicago when Darcy was in the sixth grade. As soon as she met Stephanie and Allie at John Muir Middle School, the three of them became an inseparable trio.

Darcy's theory was that they all balanced one another. Stephanie thought they were just incredibly lucky.

"What do *you* think?" Darcy asked Stephanie. "Should I get the one about the haunted pizza parlor or the one about the teen detective who investigates all her cases on Rollerblades?"

"Maybe I'm hungry, but I vote for the pizza parlor." Allie patted her stomach and laughed.

"I'd go for the Rollerblades," Stephanie said. "But, actually, I think this is the book we ought to be reading."

"How to Make Award-Winning Videos." Darcy read the title aloud.

"The book is exactly what we need," Stephanie said. "It gives you every step for making a video news show."

Darcy glanced at the book's glossy cover and

pointed at the subtitle. "Steph, it says it's for in-vestigative documentaries. You know, big, serious shows. We're just doing two- and three-minute re-ports about stuff that goes on in school."

Stephanie frowned. Stephanie, Darcy, and Allie had all signed up for a special after-school pro-gram, a three-week course in video journalism. The goal of the class was to produce a half-hour daily news show for John Muir Middle School.

Stephanie thought about having a career in jour-nalism someday, so she intended to be very serious about the class. Even if her friends weren't.

"That doesn't mean that we can't learn from the pros," Stephanie insisted. "This book is probably filled with all sorts of tips and advice that will be really useful."

Darcy looked doubtful, but didn't argue. She glanced at her watch. "We'd better get going," she said. "I'm supposed to be home for dinner in twenty minutes." She put one of the mystery nov-els back on the shelf. "And speaking of dinner, I think I will get the book about the pizza parlor mystery."

"I decided on my book half an hour ago," Allie added. "World of romance, here I come."

"Okay, I'll get the video book," Stephanie said.

Stephanie knew a little bit about television pro-duction from her dad. He and her aunt Becky were co-hosts and producers for the morning TV show, *Wake Up, San Francisco.*

Ever since Ms. Blith had announced the John Muir after-school program, Stephanie imagined herself being the producer of the news show they were going to do. She was sure she had what it took to put a TV program together. Whatever she didn't know, she could look up in the book.

Stephanie was the first one in line at the cash register. When she opened her wallet, her heart sank. "I can't believe it," she moaned. "This book costs nineteen ninety-nine. And all I have is four dollars and thirty-two cents."

"That's because you just bought sunglasses," Allie reminded her.

"Oh, right," Stephanie murmured. She did love her new sunglasses, but now all she could think about was making the video news show. She was so excited about it. And she had found the perfect book to help her get started. Now that book was about to slip out of her hands.

The woman behind the cash register glared at Stephanie. "Are you going to buy this or not?" she asked impatiently.

"I guess I can't," Stephanie said.

"Yes, you can," Darcy spoke up. "I'll just put it on my credit card."

"Or I can put it on mine," Allie chimed in. "You can pay us back when you get your allowance."

"Totally cool! You guys are great. Thanks." Stephanie smiled. She was grateful that her friends were making it possible for her to get the book she wanted so badly.

She was also embarrassed. The phrase "when you get your allowance" somehow made her feel like her nine-year-old sister, Michelle.

If Darcy's and Allie's parents could trust them to have their own credit cards, Stephanie reasoned, then her father ought to do the same. I'll ask him tomorrow, Stephanie decided. And I'll get him to say yes.

CHAPTER
2

◆ ◀ ◆ ◆

Brrring! Stephanie alarm's went off at 7:15 the next morning. A second later the clock radio's music alarm kicked in and a disc jockey's cheerful voice said, "And now, Bay Area, music to start your Monday!"

"Hey!" Stephanie's younger sister, Michelle, moaned. She rolled over in bed and pulled the blanket over her head. "Turn that thing off."

Stephanie lowered the volume on the radio, but just a little. She wanted to hear the music. It was part of her new morning ritual. She was convinced that the first song she heard each day predicted the kind of day it was going to be: good, bad, funky, or boring.

A woman's lilting voice drifted through the

6

room. "Sweet summer days," she sang. "Lazy, crazy, hot, and hazy . . ."

" 'Sweet Summer Days,' " Stephanie murmured. The song used to be a favorite of hers. She and Allie—and another girl named Maura Potter—used to play it over and over when they hung out as kids. That summer when they were going into the fourth grade, they had pajama parties and back-yard picnics almost every night. They practically wore out that one CD. It seemed to sum up every-thing they felt about summertime.

That whole summer had been a good one, Steph-anie remembered. Which meant that today was going to be a very good day.

Stephanie sat straight up as she realized—of course it was going to be a good day! The school video-journalism program started that afternoon. Last night, before she went to sleep, Stephanie read the first ten pages of her new book. It was only the introduction, but it was totally exciting. She felt as if she were about to step through a doorway into a whole new world of possibilities.

For once, she couldn't wait to get to school.

Stephanie's long blond hair swung out behind her as she raced to get dressed. She threw open her closet door. It slammed against the wall.

"Keep it down!" Michelle snapped. She rolled over in bed. "Some of us are trying to sleep around here."

Michelle's school started half an hour later than

Stephanie's. So Michelle always got up a half hour later—and she hated waking up before then.

"Okay, okay! Sorry!" Stephanie quietly shut the closet. There was nothing like sharing your bedroom with a grouchy nine-year-old lazybones, she thought. Especially when you were trying to get dressed in the morning.

Stephanie pulled on a pair of khaki shorts and a light blue polo shirt. Her thoughts quickly returned to her video-journalism class. She was already a reporter for *The Scribe*, the school paper, so she knew that she was good at identifying a news story and reporting it in an interesting way.

Working on TV stories, though, seemed like it would be a lot more fun. Everything would be faster, more visual, more like real life. Somehow working on a TV program seemed sophisticated. It sounded like a more grown-up activity than working on a school paper.

Speaking of grown-up things, I have to get started on my credit card crusade, Stephanie thought. *Hey! I should tell Dad I'm working on a TV show! Then he'll know I'm getting more mature. And maybe then he'll be willing to give me my own credit card. Just like D.J. and Darcy and Allie.*

D.J. was Stephanie's eighteen-year-old sister. She was a freshman at a nearby college. This semester she was taking extra courses in film studies. Stephanie remembered how impressed her father had been when D.J. showed him her schedule. The very next week he gave D.J. her own credit card.

Stephanie hurried downstairs to get breakfast. Danny, her dad, was already in the kitchen. He wiped the counter, attacking stains Stephanie couldn't even see. Everyone in the Tanner house knew Danny was a bit of a neat freak.

"Hi, Dad," Stephanie called. She leaned over and examined the counter. "I think you missed a spot."

"I did?" Her father peered closely at the counter, too.

"Yeah." Stephanie giggled. "But you'd need a microscope to find it."

"You're in a good mood this morning," her father observed. "Hmmm. I wonder why." He tapped his chin with his finger. "Don't tell me, let me guess—Michelle thanked you for waking her up extra early this morning."

Stephanie rolled her eyes. "Dream on." She sighed. "Sometimes, I can't helping thinking how nice it would be to have my own room."

"Well, you will this summer," her father said. "When Michelle goes to camp."

"That's true," Stephanie agreed. "I guess it's better than nothing."

Although she loved their house, it always seemed crowded. That was because eight people shared it. First there was the Tanner family—Stephanie, Michelle, D.J., and Danny.

Then there were Stephanie's uncle Jesse, his wife,

9

Becky, and their four-year-old twin sons, Nicky and Alex. Then came Danny's friend Joey, who was like another uncle to Stephanie and her sisters.

Years ago, when Stephanie's mother died, Joey and Jesse moved in with the Tanners to help Danny out. It was supposed to be a temporary arrangement, but they all quickly became one big, happy family. None of them could bear the idea of anyone moving out.

Stephanie pulled a box of Cheerios off the top shelf. Dozens of tiny Os scattered across the floor.

Stephanie examined the box. She frowned, puzzled. "Someone cut a hole in the side of the box," she said, mystified.

"Probably one of the twins," her father said. "I think Nicky was talking about wanting to have a picture on the box."

Stephanie emptied the remaining cereal into a bowl and began to pour on the milk.

She stopped the carton in midair. Milk dribbled over the sides. "Wait a minute," Stephanie said. "I just realized—you're not supposed to be home!" She checked the clock. "It's seven-thirty. Why aren't you at work?"

Wake Up, San Francisco, the TV program Danny hosted with Aunt Becky, began at seven every morning. Usually, they were both out of the house by five.

"I'm not on-air today or the next few weeks," Danny explained. "So I didn't have to go in. Becky and I have a special assignment over the next couple of weeks."

"What is it?" Stephanie asked, totally interested.

"We'll be away for a week or so, on location, shooting all over the United States and Canada. We're going to tape segments on where people in the Bay Area can spend their summer vacations."

"Oh," Stephanie said. She lowered her head over her cereal.

"Why the long face?" Danny asked.

"It's just that my special video-journalism class is starting today," Stephanie said. "And I hoped I would be able to come to you and Becky for advice."

Her father smiled. "Don't worry, you still can. We'll both be checking in, and—" He stopped. "Did you say a video-journalism class?"

Stephanie smiled. She could hear the excitement in her father's voice. "Yes. It's a special three-week program," she explained. "We meet after school and work on producing a half-hour daily TV show for the last week of school. We'll be doing up-to-the-minute newscasts about school *and* local events."

"That's fantastic," her father said. "You'll get some valuable professional experience."

Wow! This conversation was going even better than Stephanie had hoped. It was definitely time to mention that only motivated, responsible, mature students were taking the video class.

Credit card summer, here I come! Stephanie thought. Look out, world, Stephanie Tanner is ready to charge!

She put on a serious face. "The video class is part of an important program to teach kids about different careers. There will be a law class and a finance course, too.

"For our class, Ms. Blith borrowed a really good video camera and an editing machine from the Board of Education. Plus I bought a book about making video news reports. I wanted to know as much as I could before the class started."

Stephanie spooned up the last of her cereal and peered over the bowl at her dad. What was his reaction? Did he understand this was a new Stephanie? A new, mature, responsible Stephanie?

"I am so proud of you, honey," Danny said. "You're thinking about the future. *And* you're following in my footsteps!"

Stephanie grinned. "I feel more mature already."

"I'm sure you are," her father said.

Now was her chance, Stephanie was sure of it. "Hey, Dad. Think I'm mature enough for my own credit card?" she asked.

Her father's enthusiastic expression vanished. "Whoa, Steph. Where did that come from?" he said slowly.

"Well, Darcy's and Allie's parents gave them their own credit cards. And D.J. has *her* own credit card," Stephanie pointed out. "I was wondering if I could get one, too."

"D.J. is eighteen years old," her father reminded her. "And she just got one this year. Being responsible for your own credit card is a very big step. I certainly didn't give D.J. one when she was your age. I think thirteen is a bit too young."

"I agree," Michelle said. She sat down at the table.

Stephanie shot her a warning look. "But I'm a very *mature* thirteen," she argued.

"That may be," her father admitted, "but your track record hasn't been so great lately. I seem to remember you forgetting your chores last month, and ignoring Michelle when she needed homework help a while back. Neither one of those scored too high on the Tanner responsibility meter."

"Dad, those were moments of weakness. I'll never do it again!" Stephanie said. "I'm—" Stephanie's gaze shifted for a second to the kitchen clock.

Yikes! Was it 7:50 already?

"I'm going to be late for school!" she yelped, jumping out of her seat.

Danny nodded. "You'd better hurry. We can talk about the credit card later."

Stephanie started out of the kitchen.

"Wait!" Danny shouted after her. "Didn't you forget something?"

Stephanie turned back and noticed her dirty

bowl, some spilled milk, and a trail of Cheerios on the counter.

"Oops!" Stephanie darted back into the kitchen. She grabbed a sponge and mopped up the milk, then washed out her bowl.

Danny stood over her, his arms folded. He smiled. "Seems like you've got a long way to go toward becoming responsible, Steph."

"I'm sorry, Dad," Stephanie apologized. She had the sinking feeling that the chance for her own credit card was vanishing fast. Then she had an idea.

"There must be something I can do to show you how responsible I am," she said. "Maybe I can help out around here while you and Aunt Becky are on assignment for the show?"

"Actually . . ." Danny thought out loud. "There is something . . ."

"Anything!" Stephanie insisted. "Just name it!"

"How about helping Michelle get ready for camp?" he suggested.

"Sure." Stephanie agreed eagerly. *How tough could packing a few things be?* she thought. "And if I do a good job, would you *please, please* think about the credit card again?"

"We'll see," Danny replied. "For now, here's my to-do list."

He took a small piece of paper out of his pocket and handed it to Stephanie.

Stephanie's blue eyes widened as she unfolded

it and saw that it was not one page but *three full pages* of tasks. The first two pages contained an endless list of clothes, camping gear, and personal items that Michelle would need.

The final page contained orders to *Sew or adhere name tag labels on EVERYTHING* and then to neatly fold and pack it all into one trunk according to the diagram that was drawn below.

"I can't believe this," Stephanie said. "This is enough stuff to survive in the wilderness for a year!"

"I know," her father said with a shrug. "But it's what the camp says every camper must have, so we've got to go along with it." He patted Stephanie on the shoulder. "It's going to be a lot easier now that you've volunteered to help."

Stephanie nodded and forced a smile. What in the world had she just gotten herself into?

Then she remembered. This was going to help prove to her father how responsible she was. Responsible enough to get a credit card. Her own credit card. Having it would make all this hard work worth it.

CHAPTER
3

♦ ◄ ▪ ♦

"Steph!" Allie waved to Stephanie as she came out of her last class that afternoon. "Over here!"

Stephanie joined Allie at her locker. Darcy bounded toward them from the opposite end of the hall. "Hey, guys! Ready for video-journalism?"

"You bet," Allie called.

"I sure am." Stephanie nodded.

The girls all spun the combinations on their lockers and gathered the books they would need to take home. Then they slammed the doors shut and set off for the media arts room together.

"So." Allie poked Stephanie's shoulder. "Do you think the world of TV journalism is ready for us?"

"It better be," Stephanie said. "I am so psyched for this class."

"I am, too," Darcy said. "It's going to be so cool

to make a TV show." She tossed her hair, flashed a smile, and joked, "I think I'd make an excellent on-camera reporter."

"Sure, if your ego fits on the screen!" Stephanie joked.

"Hey." Darcy laughed. She swatted at Stephanie with her notebook.

Allie gave a little shudder. "I'll be much happier with a job *behind* the camera," she commented. "What about you, Steph? Do you think you'll be writing the scripts, like you write articles for *The Scribe*?"

"I don't know," Stephanie said. "I love writing, but I'd kind of like to try something—different." *Like running the entire production,* Stephanie added to herself.

Suddenly a loud bang echoed down the hall. Stephanie turned to see a girl in a long, plaid skirt pick up a bunch of heavy textbooks from the floor.

It's Maura, Stephanie thought. *That figures.*

"Way to go, Potter!" someone called to the girl. A few lockers away, a boy dropped his books on the floor, imitating her. A bunch of kids snickered and laughed.

Maura gathered her books, not seeming to notice any of the teasing that was going on around her.

Stephanie watched as Maura slid the books into a tattered army surplus bag, slung the bag over her shoulder, then headed down the hall. Some-

17

how, she paid no attention to the loud giggles and whispers that followed her.

Stephanie shook her head. If anyone laughed at her like that, she'd die of humiliation.

The tune to "Sweet Summer Days" ran through Stephanie's head. She sighed softly. She and Maura had been such good friends. If only Maura hadn't changed, hadn't become so . . . weird.

She always wore strange clothes now, things that looked like they came from the Salvation Army. And she was *so* shy. She never went to any of the school games or pep rallies or dances.

At lunch she always sat by herself, reading. Stephanie once noticed one of Maura's notebooks in passing. The girl didn't even doodle during class. Instead, she filled the margins of her pages with poems written in a tiny, scrunched-up handwriting.

When did it happen? Stephanie wondered. When had Maura changed? How had she become so different from everyone else?

The halls grew quiet as most everyone left school for the day. Darcy tugged on Stephanie's arm. "Let's go," she said.

Stephanie snapped back to reality. The video-journalism class. They didn't want to be late on the first day.

She, Darcy, and Allie ran into the media arts room. Stephanie glanced around at the students assembled there. "Hi, guys," she said, pleased to see a lot of her friends from John Muir's school paper, *The Scribe.*

There were about a dozen people altogether and not many empty seats. Stephanie slipped into a chair next to Gia Mactavish, *The Scribe*'s photographer. Darcy and Allie settled into chairs behind her.

"I can't wait to try out the new camcorder for this newscast," Gia said. "It'll be so cool to learn how to use a real news camera!"

"I know," Sue Kramer, the editor of *The Scribe,* spoke up from across the room. "It'll be a totally new take on the news."

Bill Klepper shook his head. "Not a totally new take," he said. "We're still reporting. Being truthful, accurate, and objective. It's just a different way of *presenting* it."

Stephanie rolled her eyes. "There they go again," she said softly to Gia. Gia stifled a giggle.

Bill and Sue used to date. Stephanie thought that since they stopped dating, they disagreed with each other just to disagree.

The classroom door swung wide open and banged loudly against the wall. A second later Tiffany Schroeder strode into the room. With her nose in the air, she surveyed the scene.

"Oh, no," Darcy groaned. "Flamingo alert!"

"Great," Stephanie whispered. "Just what we need."

The Flamingoes were a clique of the snobbiest girls in the school. Everyone who was a member of the Flamingoes was pretty and popular—and they all wore pink. They also liked to cause trouble for Stephanie and her friends because they didn't want to be a part of the stuck-up group.

Tiffany plopped down into a seat next to Allie. She took out a pocket mirror and ran a hand through her long hair.

Then she tapped Gia on the back. "Which do you think is my best side?" she asked.

Before Gia could answer, Ms. Blith walked into the room. Ms. Blith was the adviser for the *Scribe*. She had worked as a local TV journalist before she became a teacher at John Muir.

Stephanie thought Ms. Blith was the best—she gave the students lots of freedom, so that they could learn as much as possible. But she was always there to answer their questions, too.

"This is the start of an experimental video TV program," Ms. Blith began. "During this last month of school, we're going to produce a news program for John Muir. If we're successful, the school will consider offering a video program as part of its regular after-school activities. So what happens next year depends on what we do in the next three weeks."

Wow! That means this course is even more important than I thought. And it makes me look even more responsible, Stephanie realized. I have to remember to mention this to Dad.

Ms. Blith raised her hand for silence. Then she slipped a tape into the VCR.

"What's going on?" Allie asked softly.

Stephanie shrugged. Was it a tape of a newscast? A kind of model for them to use?

The TV blinked on, and Ms. Blith came on-screen. She was holding a copy of *The Scribe*. Without lifting her head, Ms. Blith began to read the headlines of the news items.

" 'Volunteer Clean-Up Crew to Maintain School Grounds,' " she read. " 'Gym Closed for Painting. Art Class Visits Museum. Basketball Team Wins Again.' "

Stephanie stifled a yawn. She actually wrote one or two of those articles. But when the headlines were read out loud like that, they seemed kind of . . . well, boring.

On-screen, Ms. Blith stopped reading. She lifted her head and gazed squarely into the camera. "Your challenge is to make this kind of material more exciting."

Stephanie's mind began to whir. Obviously, newspaper techniques didn't work on camera. The first thing she needed to think about was the differences between the two media.

"Ms. Blith," she said, raising her hand. "I think I can tell why that newscast didn't work."

"Good. Give it a try, Stephanie," Ms. Blith said, encouraging her.

"Those headlines sound fine when you're reading them to yourself," Stephanie said. "But you have to consider that you're reading them to an audience. They need more drama, more explanation, so the audience will be entertained."

"I thought the basketball one sounded just fine," Josh Linder joked. Everyone laughed. Josh was on the basketball team.

"Anything with the word *basketball* in it sounds exciting to you," Darcy teased.

Ms. Blith smiled. "You're on the right track, Stephanie. It's not a good idea to just transfer print into video. Even though we will be calling this newscast *Scribe TV*."

"We're going to need a completely different approach," Stephanie said, thinking aloud.

"Exactly," Ms. Blith agreed.

"To start with," Stephanie went on, "everything we report has got to have a visual. That's a graphic image that goes with the story. It's meant to catch the viewer's attention. It could be a photograph or a chart or—"

"How do *you* know so much about it?" Tiffany interrupted.

Stephanie shrugged. "I've read about it. And I've watched a lot of news shows. Not to mention that my dad *hosts* a TV news show. I can pretty much tell what works and what doesn't."

She thought for a second, then went on. "With TV, the audience isn't reading the news stories on their own, so the reporters have to make the stories sound exciting and immediate. Like a friend is in the room, telling you about this really exciting, important event."

Ms. Blith nodded. "Absolutely. When you write for TV you always have to remember that the text is going to be spoken. You need to keep that in mind as you decide which stories to cover."

Tiffany spoke up in a sarcastic voice. "I'm sure Stephanie has already figured out which stories she wants to cover. And she probably wants to *write* them all, too."

"Not really," Stephanie admitted. "Actually, I thought it'd be fun to do something different for TV. What I'd really like to do is . . ." Stephanie hoped it wouldn't sound conceited, but she was just too excited to hold back. "I want to be the producer," she said.

"The producer?" Ms. Blith repeated slowly. "That's a lot of hard work, Stephanie. Do you know what's involved?"

"Sure," Stephanie answered. She remembered what it said in the first chapter of the book she'd bought. "The producer comes up with the basic plan for the show, then makes sure all the parts work together smoothly."

"To tell you the truth," Ms. Blith said, "I wasn't planning on having a student producer. I—"

"I know there's a lot to coordinate," Stephanie said, "but I'm sure I could do a really good job of it."

"Well, we have to move quickly," Ms. Blith warned. "We need the show up and running in a very few weeks." She looked at Stephanie doubtfully. "Being producer of the newscast is a lot of responsibility for one person."

Excellent! I want to do everything I can for Scribe TV, *plus I want to prove to my dad just how responsible I am,* Stephanie thought. *This will let me do both.*

"I have experience," Stephanie told Ms. Blith. "I even worked at the studio where my dad films his show for a while."

"Yeah," Darcy chimed in. "Making coffee."

Stephanie blushed. "Well, yes. I *did* make coffee. But I also learned from watching," she added quickly. "So what do you think, Ms. Blith? Can I be producer?"

"You'll *all* need to think about your job assignments," Ms. Blith told the class, not answering Stephanie either way. "What kind of work would you like to do? What are you most suited for? Right now, though, we should brainstorm. Figure out what direction we want to take for tone and style."

"Oh, I know all about that," Stephanie assured the class. "On my dad's show they're very relaxed but professional. My dad and my aunt Becky start out each show with a little chat and then . . ."

Stephanie explained the format of *Wake Up, San Francisco,* and then talked about how it compared with the other local news shows. She knew she might be talking more than the other kids, but the video project was so exciting, she couldn't help herself. Besides, if she was going to be producer, she'd have to take charge of discussions anyway. This was kind of like practice.

Stephanie was just giving her opinion on a local late night newscast when Ms. Blith signaled that the class was over. Stephanie turned to Darcy and Allie. "I feel so pumped about this project. Why don't you come over to my house and we can talk more tonight?"

"You mean *all* of us will talk?" Darcy teased. "Or will the two of us just listen to *you*?"

Allie grinned as they left the media arts room. "Maybe we should come prepared to take notes." She switched into a mock TV announcer's voice. "And tonight a special evening with Stephanie Tanner: *Everything You Always Wanted to Know About Television but Were Too Sane to Ask.*"

"Okay, okay," Stephanie said. "I'm sorry if I acted like some sort of expert. I guess I just got carried away. I'm so excited about putting this program together. I know I could do a terrific news show."

"You are *so* wrong," a voice said behind her. Stephanie whirled around and saw Tiffany, the Flamingo, standing there.

"What do you mean, I'm so wrong?" Stephanie asked.

"Well, look at you," Tiffany said. "You're wearing khaki shorts and a blue polo shirt. I mean, your clothes say it all. You're okay—but plain, unimaginative, and totally un-hip. There's no way you can put together a TV show that's going to be interesting to the kids at John Muir."

Stephanie felt her blood boil. "For your information, Tiffany, I *am* going to be named producer of this show. And I am going to make sure *Scribe TV* is the hippest, coolest show ever!"

CHAPTER
4

♦ ◄ ♦ ♦

At dinner that night Stephanie couldn't stop talking about *Scribe TV*.

Only Uncle Jesse and the twins were at the table with her. Danny and Becky were working late, getting ready for their trip for *Wake Up, San Francisco*. Michelle was eating at her friend Rachel's house. D.J. was at the college library, and Joey had a date.

"So," Stephanie said. She twirled some spaghetti around her fork. "This video project could be the biggest thing to hit John Muir since computers. Don't you think I'd make a good producer?"

"No!" Jesse said.

"No?" Stephanie repeated, surprised.

"No, Nicky! Don't!" Jesse begged. But the four-year-old flicked his meatball off his fork, right into the garbage pail.

"Two points!" Nicky cried.

"This is *the most exciting thing* ever," Stephanie explained. "It's a chance to show—"

Alex, the other twin, flicked his meatball, too. But he missed the garbage can. The meatball landed on the floor with a gross *splat*.

"Boys!" Jesse scolded. "You *eat* dinner. You don't shoot hoops with it."

"Uncle Jesse," Stephanie pleaded. "I'm trying to tell you about this project!"

"I know. I'm listening, Steph," Jesse said. He turned his back on her to scoop Alex into his chair. "It's just—come back," he yelled as Nicky bolted off toward the refrigerator.

"Never mind," Stephanie said with a sigh.

She ate her dinner and tried to keep the twins from getting into too much trouble. Then she cleared her plate from the table and went up to her room.

On her bed she saw a pile of Michelle's clothing. Stephanie shook her head. Michelle was always leaving her stuff all over the room.

Then Stephanie realized that the pile was too neat for Michelle to have left it there. She spied an envelope sitting on the top of the pile. Her name was written on the envelope. Inside, Stephanie found name tags, a needle and thread, and a note.

Steph—

Michelle will be taking all this stuff to camp.
Any help you can give me on sewing in name
tags would be great.

Love,
Dad

Stephanie stared at the pile—underwear, T-shirts,
jeans, sweats.

Whoa! Too much stuff. She couldn't deal with
all of that just then.

Instead, she flopped down on her comforter and
started to read a little more in the book about producing video news programs.

The first chapter was about drawing up a budget
for the show. Stephanie knew she wouldn't need
to do that. Ms. Blith already had a budget from
the school. She skipped ahead to the next chapter.

" 'How to Insure Your Production Properly,' "
Steph read aloud. Looked like that chapter didn't
apply to her either. She flipped to the next chapter
on—research teams?

Stephanie closed the book with a snap. This
wasn't helping her at all. She supposed she could
start her homework, but it seemed so dull. The
video-journalism program was definitely the most
important thing in her life, and she simply had to
talk to someone about it.

She quickly dialed Allie's number. Allie had three-way calling. Stephanie figured Allie could dial Darcy, and all three of them could talk at once.

The phone rang four times, then Stephanie heard a click. "Hello, there's no one home right now. . . ." The message came on. "Hey, Al," Stephanie said after the beep. "Call me right away. We need to talk about the project."

Then she tried to call Darcy, but no one was home at her house, either.

Stephanie sat near the phone waiting for Darcy and Allie to return her calls all evening. The phone never rang.

After Michelle was long asleep, Stephanie glanced at the clock: 10:02. It was too late for her friends to call. With a sigh she picked up one of Michelle's T-shirts and began sewing in the first name tag.

The next day, before school started, Stephanie waited for her friends at their usual meeting place, the pay phone near the gym.

Soon she spotted them walking slowly down the hall. Stephanie could see that they were studying something in a teen magazine.

"Hey," Stephanie called out. "What's up?"

Darcy looked up. "Hi, Steph. We're trying to decide on a new hairstyle for me. I'm wondering if I should get a really short cut."

"Definitely not," Allie said. "I love your hair long!"

"I think it'd look great either way," Stephanie said honestly. Then she asked the question that was bugging her, "Where were you two last night?"

"My parents and I went to that new Italian restaurant, Pasta LaVista," Allie said.

"Oh, how was it?" Darcy asked. "We went out for dinner last night, too, but my mom wanted Chinese food."

"Well," Allie began, "it was—"

"Excuse me," Stephanie interrupted, trying to stay calm. "But didn't anyone get my messages last night?"

"Sure," Allie said. "But I got home too late to call back."

"I didn't want to call and wake Michelle or the twins," Darcy said.

"I wanted to talk about the video project," Stephanie explained. "You know, brainstorm more ideas. Don't you guys care about this at all? Where are your priorities?"

"Priorities?" Darcy repeated, confused. "We just had one class so far. How could it be a priority yet?"

"Okay, maybe we met only once," Stephanie said. "But don't you think it's the most exciting thing going on in this entire school?"

"I guess it's got potential," Allie said.

"Steph, aren't you taking this TV thing a little too seriously—" Darcy began. But she was interrupted by the first-period bell.

"We'd better talk about this later," Allie said, and the three girls went to their separate classes.

All that day Stephanie kept imagining what it would be like to be the producer of *Scribe TV*. She loved the idea of running the news show, the hottest thing going at John Muir. It would be a chance to use everything she had learned about telling a good story—and to use it in a new, exciting way. At the same time, she'd prove to her father that she was totally responsible.

Scribe TV might change her life in other ways, too. Maybe the show would be good enough to be picked up by a local TV station. Stephanie had no trouble imagining her name rolling by on the credits of the evening news. She actually spent her lunch period watching the midday news in the dark, dusty audiovisual-aids room. By the time she entered the media arts room after school, Stephanie was so fired up, she could hardly sit still.

She fidgeted impatiently as Ms. Blith explained that they were going to produce several thirty-minute shows, made up of two- and three-minute stories. "So we need a lot of material for this one show," the adviser said. "We're going to need news stories and other features as well. This is *your* TV show, so think about the kinds of information that might be useful to you."

Stephanie and a few others raised their hands. Ms. Blith called on Allie.

"How about having a bulletin board on-screen?"

Allie suggested. "To post jobs. It'd be perfect with summer coming up."

Stephanie pictured a plain old bulletin board with pushpins and little notes. Boring, she decided.

"Sorry, Allie," Stephanie said. "But we need more excitement. Just looking at a bulletin board is too static." She didn't want her friend to feel bad, but she knew that if she were going to be producer, she had to make her views known without playing favorites. "We need something a little jazzier."

"How about sports stats?" Darcy offered. "We could have them constantly running along the bottom of the screen. We could show scores of school games, and maybe even statistics for the whole season. Or even John Muir team trivia—"

"Who would read stuff like that?" Stephanie broke in.

"I would," Josh said.

"So would I," said Gia. "And I think we ought to do specials on some of the students. Profiles. You know, there's that seventh-grader who just won a major chess tournament."

"Chess is history," Stephanie said. "They've got computers now that can beat humans. Five years from now, no one will even bother to play."

Quentin Baglio raised his hand. Stephanie didn't know much about Quentin except that he was a seventh-grader and a total computer nerd. "I think we should have a weather report," he said.

"How accurate could it be?" Stephanie asked. "It's not like John Muir has its own weather satellite."

"I can download reports from the Internet," Quentin said.

"Anything else?" Ms. Blith said. "Any other ideas?"

The room was silent. People seemed a little hesitant to speak up.

"I've got an idea," Tiffany finally said. She fluffed her hair and waited for everyone to look her way. "We can show how the anchorpeople get made up before every newscast. Viewers would be fascinated to see how I—I mean the anchor—gets to look so terrific.

"Or," Tiffany went on, "we can feature the Flamingoes, and our everyday activities. I know, we could have a pink set to match our clothes."

Stephanie and Darcy exchanged a glance. "Pink?" Stephanie said. "That would look like we're not serious newspeople."

"That's true," Sue agreed. She shot a hesitant look at Stephanie. "Maybe we could have a classroom setting. That would be easy enough, and would seem like we mean business."

"A regular classroom is too dull," Stephanie said. "Kids would just tune us out."

"Let's *not* have a set," Bill suggested. "Let's keep the show real loose. Have it be different every time."

"That's too loose," Stephanie said. "I remember my father and my aunt Becky went through this exact same thing with their show. A show has to have some sort of home base."

"Well," Darcy put in. "Since you seem to know everything, Steph, what do *you* think the set should look like?"

Stephanie paused. She'd been so busy considering other people's ideas, she hadn't come up with any of her own.

"Wellll." She drew out the word to stall for time. "I like a traditional news set. Gray everything, with a long desk and a clock behind it. Like you see on the news every night."

Tiffany stifled a yawn. Stephanie knew it wasn't the most thrilling idea, but at least it made sense.

Miss Blith glanced at her watch. "I'm sorry, people," she said. "It's four-thirty and I've got to leave early today. We'll discuss this in more detail tomorrow. So think things over carefully."

The last school bus of the day had already left, so Stephanie, Allie, and Darcy walked to one of the city bus stops together. Actually, Darcy and Allie were walking together. Stephanie trailed a few feet behind.

"Hey, what's the rush?" Stephanie hurried to keep up as her friends strode ahead. She drew alongside them. "So what did you think of video class? Can you believe some of those ideas!"

"The ideas were fine," Darcy said. "*You* were the problem."

"Me?" Stephanie asked, surprised.

"Well," Allie said, "you acted like you were in charge. You shot down every single idea."

"I was just trying to be a producer," Stephanie explained.

"Excuse me," Darcy said, "but I don't remember Ms. Blith saying you had the job. I don't remember anyone making you boss."

"Well, no one did officially," Stephanie admitted. "But someone has to step in and do the job. This is *our* project. Ms. Blith shouldn't be doing anything but guiding us."

"Maybe," Allie said. "But that doesn't give you the right to say our ideas won't work. What's wrong with posting jobs and sports stats, anyway?"

Stephanie realized that Allie and Darcy were hurt. "Look, maybe I could have been a little more diplomatic," she said. "But I still say the show needs something . . . different. I know I'm right," she insisted.

"Well, I know you're stubborn," Darcy retorted. "And it's not like you came up with any awesome, creative things, either."

Stephanie grumbled. She couldn't give in to her friends. Not with so much riding on the project . . .

She imagined her father watching their finished newscasts and saying, "That's incredible, Steph. I didn't realize you had so much talent. Or that you were so responsible and together. I guess you do deserve your own credit card, after all. And let's talk about giving you your own network TV show . . ."

"Listen," Stephanie said. "I just think we have an incredible opportunity here. This show could be so amazing. I mean, it could change our lives . . . if only you'd work at it a little."

Darcy and Allie stopped in their tracks.

"You think we're not working hard enough?" Allie said.

"I didn't mean that exactly." Stephanie fumbled for words. "I meant, if only you'd see things my way . . ."

"Steph," Allie said, "I have to tell you that you're being completely ridiculous."

"Ridiculous?" Stephanie repeated. She felt her face flush bright red. "Can't you understand how important this is to me? Can't you support me on this?"

"We want to, Steph, but not when you won't even consider any of our suggestions," Darcy said calmly. She and Allie exchanged a meaningful look. "Give us a call when you cool off a bit," she finished.

Then they turned around and started to walk home, leaving Stephanie at the bus stop.

Alone.

CHAPTER
5

◆ ◀ ◆ ◆

"Some friends they are," Stephanie grumbled. She trudged the last few steps to the bus stop. "Doesn't anyone understand that I'm pushing so hard because I want the show to be great?"

Stephanie stopped at the bench under the bus shelter. Only one other person was waiting for the bus—Maura Potter.

Stephanie noticed her fiddling with the buttons on her Walkman. Steph took a seat and settled in to wait for the bus, when Maura started *dancing!*

Stephanie couldn't believe it! But there Maura was, dancing to music that no one could hear. It looked so funny that Stephanie had to bite her tongue to keep from laughing.

She watched as Maura moved strangely. Waving

her arms slowly, like she was floating through clouds.

Maura is *definitely* odd, Stephanie thought. She wondered how long it had been since they'd really talked. Probably not since fifth grade. She didn't remember when exactly they stopped being friends. All she knew for certain was that now, as far as ninety percent of John Muir was concerned, hanging out with Maura Potter was totally un-cool.

Still, Stephanie wondered, should she say hello? They *had* been friends for so long. Stephanie glanced left, then right. No one else was around.

Why not? Stephanie reasoned. She cleared her throat—loudly. Maura froze in place. She peeked over her shoulder and noticed Stephanie. A bright red blush crept across her cheeks.

"Whoops! Sorry about the dance routine," Maura said, staring at the sidewalk. "I didn't know anyone was there. And I was really getting into my Cure tape."

Stephanie nodded, giving a little half-smile. Maura looked up and smiled back, still a little unsure.

"You're leaving school late," she said to Stephanie. "Are you in that new after-school program?"

"I'm taking the video-journalism course," Stephanie said.

"I'm taking a class, too. A poetry workshop, at the Y across the street. It's only me and four other people." Maura paused. "It's really interesting, though."

Stephanie remembered that Maura had always liked to write. She'd never gone out for *The Scribe*, though. Maura wanted to write only poetry.

Maura nodded toward Darcy and Allie, who were walking off in the other direction. "Is everything okay with you guys?"

"It wasn't anything, really," Stephanie explained. "Just a silly argument over our video project."

"Oh," Maura said. "What are your newscasts going to be like, anyway?"

"We're not really sure yet," Stephanie admitted. "Not a whole lot has been decided so far. But I'll probably be producer. We're working on the look of the show now. I think we'll go with a traditional set. You know. Desk. Clock. The works."

Maura gazed at the sidewalk again. Her long hair fell in front of her eyes. "Are you sure you want to go with 'traditional'?" she asked softly. "The kids at John Muir are hip. They're wired into MTV. Most of them are on-line. They might want to see something a little more cutting-edge." She paused, waiting for Stephanie's reaction.

My ideas aren't hip enough, Stephanie thought.

That was sort of what Tiffany had said. But coming from Maura, Stephanie sensed no meanness in the criticism. Hmmm, Stephanie thought. Maybe Maura has a point.

"What kind of cutting-edge stuff do you mean?" Stephanie asked.

"You know what would be totally cool?" Maura spoke more quickly now, more sure of herself. "If you had a really funky set—like at a special table in the cafeteria. And if you had all sorts of decorations behind you. You know, music posters, movie posters. All tacked up in different, weird ways."

"Some of them could be ripped or wrinkled," Stephanie said, catching on to the idea.

"Exactly!" Maura said. "Or maybe instead of a *table*, you could put a really funky couch in the cafeteria. . . ."

Maura spun out all sorts of possibilities. The more Stephanie heard, the more she liked what Maura was thinking.

Maura always *did* have fun ideas, Stephanie remembered. Like having a smoothie stand instead of a regular lemonade stand. Or putting on plays based on the books they read. Stephanie remembered a *Charlotte's Web* play, where she and Allie and Maura all argued about who got to be Wilbur the pig.

For the moment Stephanie forgot all the years when she and Maura weren't friends. She felt like they were talking the way they had summers before, lying on their backs on the grass, gazing up at the stars. . . .

Stephanie smiled at Maura, about to ask if she

remembered all those times. Just then, though, she spotted someone over Maura's shoulder.

Tiffany! Stephanie stiffened. She was headed straight for the bus stop—straight for a bird's-eye view of Stephanie, deep in conversation with Maura.

Slowly Stephanie backed away from Maura. Tiffany had the biggest mouth in school. In two seconds flat word would be out that Stephanie Tanner had a new best friend—Maura Potter. And Stephanie couldn't allow that to happen.

Everyone thought Maura was so un-cool. Stephanie would be considered un-cool, too, if they were caught hanging out together.

"You know," Stephanie interrupted Maura mid-sentence, "I think I'll walk home, it's such a nice day."

Maura stared at her, confused.

"But it was good talking to you," Stephanie added. "You really have some great ideas!"

Maura nodded. "Uh—sure, Stephanie. Anytime."

Stephanie felt a guilty pang for cutting out like that, but Tiffany was getting closer to the bus stop by the second.

"See you!" Stephanie called. She turned quickly in the direction of her street and jogged off.

She kept jogging until she was a good distance away. Then she turned to look behind her.

One question repeated in her mind: Did Tiffany see her talking to Maura?

CHAPTER
6

♦ ◄ � ♦

The next day at school Stephanie quickly knew that everything was fine. No one treated her strangely. So Tiffany must not have seen a thing.

Whew! Stephanie thought. That was a close one.

She got to school early that morning, excited about the ideas Maura had given her. Before she told anyone about them, she wanted to talk with Darcy and Allie. She found them both at Allie's locker.

"Hey, guys," Stephanie said.

"Hi," Allie replied.

"Hi," Darcy echoed.

"I wanted to tell you that I know I got a little carried away yesterday. And that I'm sorry," Stephanie said.

"*A little carried away?*" Darcy echoed.

"Okay, maybe a lot," Stephanie admitted. "I've just been so pumped about this whole video thing."

Allie looked at her curiously. "We're excited about it, too, but why does it matter *so* much to you?"

Stephanie hesitated. Should she tell them about showing her father how mature she was so she could have a credit card like they did?

No, it would be too humiliating if she *didn't* get the credit card after all.

"You know," Stephanie began, "when I started writing for *The Scribe*, everything was all set up. What the paper looks like, how long the articles are, the kinds of things we write about. But with *Scribe TV* we've got a chance to start something from scratch. It's a chance to be totally creative."

"And to do something that the whole school will really respond to," Allie said, catching her enthusiasm.

"I just want to put together something that's really great," Stephanie said.

Darcy smiled. "We will." She put her arm around Stephanie. "If we do it together!"

By the time Stephanie got to the media arts room that afternoon, she was feeling good. She'd straightened things out with Darcy and Allie, and Maura's ideas for the set were good ones.

Steph sat down next to Darcy as Ms. Blith came

into the room. "Yesterday, after you and Allie left," she began, "I was talking to—"

"Shhh!" Tiffany twisted around in her seat and glared at Stephanie. "Ms. Blith might be announcing the anchorperson, and I want to hear my name."

At the front of the room, Ms. Blith laughed. "There isn't any announcement quite yet, Tiffany. Before we get into jobs, I'd like to get back to the set."

"I've got some ideas," Stephanie spoke up.

"Shocking," Tiffany muttered under her breath.

Stephanie ignored her. She went on to tell the class Maura's ideas: about the funky look the set could have.

"That sounds really good," Allie said when Stephanie had finished.

"It is cool," Gia added. "We could all raid our attics for props. It could look like someone's living room."

"Yeah," Sue put in. "Or like a really hip coffee place."

"I think the main color should be pink," Tiffany added.

Stephanie resisted the urge to joke about Tiffany's comment. Instead, she said, "It should look like a place where *everyone* would want to hang out. Not just specific groups of people."

"And I do *not* want to hang out in pink," Josh stated.

45

"Good," Ms. Blith encouraged the staff. "Stephanie, you've given us a starting point. It sounds like what we're talking about is a look that's funky and casual. Is there anyone here who doesn't want to go with that?"

No one in the class objected. Though Stephanie did catch Tiffany glaring at her.

"Fine," Ms. Blith went on. "Now let's talk about jobs. The first thing we need is a producer. Our producer should be someone who's creative—who has a vision of how *Scribe TV* can be the most exciting thing John Muir Middle School has ever seen. Although our director will be responsible for a lot of what happens on camera, the producer coordinates everything. The producer has to be the troubleshooter and the problem solver. Do I have any nominations or volunteers?"

"I nominate Stephanie," Allie said.

"Figures," Tiffany muttered.

"Tiffany?" Ms. Blith asked. "Do you have any objection to that?"

Tiffany shook her head. "I don't want to be producer. *I* want to be *in front* of the camera."

Stephanie wondered if anyone else would oppose her.

"How about you, Sue?" Ms. Blith questioned.

"Actually, I really like Stephanie's ideas," Sue said. "And I think I might like to be in front of the camera, too."

"Fine. Anyone else?" Ms. Blith asked.

Stephanie felt her heart jump into her throat. She wanted the position so badly. What if someone else got it?

Ms. Blith waited for what seemed like hours, but no one else spoke up. Ms. Blith smiled at Stephanie. "It looks like it's unanimous. Stephanie, you're *Scribe TV*'s producer."

"Wow!" Stephanie gasped. For a moment she felt so excited, she couldn't think of anything else to say.

When she had calmed down a bit, she rose to her feet. "Thanks, everyone," she told the class. "I really appreciate you giving me this chance. And I promise to work on this newscast day and night. It will have my complete and undivided attention. Nothing will stop this from being the greatest thing John Muir Middle School has ever seen!"

The entire *Scribe TV* staff clapped and cheered for Stephanie.

Stephanie hardly remembered the bus ride home from school that afternoon. She was so happy about her position as producer that she found herself daydreaming about the future.

Scribe TV was just the beginning! She pictured herself in a fabulous job in TV journalism. Then she imagined herself stepping up to a podium. Taking a golden statue. Thanking all the little people who helped her along the way . . .

"Stephanie!" Danny's voice called.

Stephanie snapped out of her fantasy. She looked up. "Oh. Hi, Dad!"

"I asked, how's it going?" he repeated.

"Great!" Stephanie sighed happily.

"Are you making any headway on Michelle's list?"

Stephanie stopped. "Oh! You want to know how *that's* going!" Stephanie racked her brain. What had she done on Michelle's list?

"Um—I sewed on a few of the name tags," she remembered.

"Only a few?" Danny asked.

"Actually—one," Stephanie confessed.

Her father gave her a worried look. "Becky and I leave tomorrow for our location shoots," he explained. "We could be gone for a while. And I want to make sure things are moving along. You know, there are a lot of things Michelle still has to get on that list. I was hoping you were going to take her shopping."

"I am," Stephanie said quickly.

"When?" her father asked.

"Soon," Stephanie promised. She realized she hadn't set aside time for shopping at all. Besides her normal homework and chores, now she was producer. She wasn't sure if, or *when*, she could fit Michelle in. But she couldn't tell *that* to her father.

"Guess what, Dad?" she said excitedly. "I've just been named producer of *Scribe TV*!"

Danny's face lit up. He gave Stephanie a big hug.

"That's terrific! I'm so proud of you, honey." Then he thought a moment. "Hmmm. Being a producer is a tough job. And I know helping Michelle is a lot to handle. Tell you what. I'll ask D.J. to take over."

"No!" Stephanie said quickly. Having D.J. take over would make her look really immature. She had to prove to Danny that she could handle everything, so he'd know she was mature and trustworthy. And that she deserved to have her own credit card.

"I can do it all. Really," Stephanie assured him. "This school project won't take up that much time. I mean, producers distribute tasks to their staff, right? I've got a really good team. I'll manage just fine."

"Well," Danny said slowly. "If you think you can do it. . . ."

"Believe me," Stephanie told him. "I can do it. In fact, I'm going to get started right now."

Stephanie raced up the stairs to the bedroom. Inside, she found Michelle reading a book.

"Guess what?" Steph said, scanning the to-do list. "I'm taking you to the sporting goods store tomorrow after school."

"Cool," Michelle stated, not taking her eyes off her book.

Stephanie raced back downstairs. "I'm going to take Michelle to the sporting goods store tomorrow," she told him.

"Great," Danny said. "Now, I'm trusting you to

be careful with money. Remember, Michelle doesn't need high-tech, fancy gear. A cheap flashlight will work as well as an expensive one."

"Got it," Stephanie said confidently.

"I'll give you a note with my credit card so you can charge things to my account," Danny said.

"Sure, Dad," Stephanie said. "But if I had my *own* credit card, you wouldn't have to do that."

"We'll see, honey," Danny responded. "We'll see."

"You won't regret it." Stephanie smiled. "We'll get everything on the list."

CHAPTER
7

"Could I have everyone's attention, please?" Stephanie stood at the front of the noisy *Scribe TV* classroom. "Hello?"

She held up her hand for quiet, but the room grew even noisier. The class had begun that afternoon with Ms. Blith asking all the students to write down their names and the job they each wanted. Then Ms. Blith and Stephanie had a quick meeting in the hallway.

"I'm going to hand out assignments now." Stephanie yelled to be heard above everyone.

The room suddenly quieted. Everyone stared at Stephanie expectantly. She grinned. She had their complete and total attention.

Wow! she thought. I could really get into this producer business.

"Well?" Tiffany said. "Make it official, so I can figure out what I'll be wearing as anchor."

Stephanie cleared her throat. "We've decided Bill and Sue will be co-anchors."

"Huh?" Tiffany gasped.

Bill and Sue gave each other high-fives. It looked as if they were agreeing on something, finally. Stephanie hoped it wouldn't last long. She was counting on their quarreling to heat up the newscast.

"Wait, Tiffany," Stephanie said. "You haven't heard *your* assignment yet. You'll be health and beauty reporter."

"Just a reporter? What's so great about that?" Tiffany asked suspiciously.

"Not just any reporter. You'll be in charge of the segments all the really popular girls will be dying to see. You know, all about makeup, clothing, getting into great shape before the summer—that kind of thing. Everyone in John Muir will consider you the ultimate word on beauty."

Tiffany brightened. "I'll take it!" she said.

Next Stephanie named Darcy sports reporter and a girl named Shawna the roving reporter. She put a boy named Eric in charge of props and set design and Gia in charge of the camera. Quentin would be the weather forecaster and Josh the director.

"Reporters will do their own writing," Stephanie concluded, "overseen by our head writer, Allie."

Allie mouthed a silent thank-you to Stephanie.

That morning she had reminded Stephanie she wanted a *behind*-the-scenes job. Steph thought this would be just perfect for her.

"All right," Miss Blith announced. "On to the next order of business—coming up with story ideas for our first newscast."

For the next hour the class broke into pairs to brainstorm more ideas. It seemed as though each pair wanted to ask Stephanie a million questions. She was pulled from group to group, trying to answer them all. Wardrobe? Content? Music?

Soon Stephanie's head was spinning. There was *so* much to decide. And she had to give her opinion on just about everything—even if she didn't have one.

"Music, music, music," Stephanie muttered to herself. What would be the best way to handle that? Have it playing all through the show? Or just to introduce each segment? What kind of music should they have? Josh had suggested Worldbeat, Sue wanted classical, Eric thought they should have his brother playing guitar in the background, and Tiffany was pushing for dance music. None of those sounded quite right to Stephanie. Though at the moment she didn't have a better idea.

Darcy dragged Stephanie off to one side. "How can we make my sportscast different?" she asked. "I don't want to just stand in front of some game, holding a microphone like everyone else does."

"Um," Stephanie mumbled, stumped for a quick

response. She stood still for a moment, hoping an idea—any idea—would pop into her head. Nothing did.

She would just stall, and later, in private, without anyone around, she'd figure out something fresh and innovative. She pulled out a notepad and scribbled in a sentence.

"I'll get right on it," she told Darcy. "Right now I'm making a list of all the decisions to be made."

"Okay," Darcy said. "But we need something funky and fun—like your ideas for the set."

Which weren't really my ideas. They came from Maura, Stephanie thought. She felt a guilty pang.

Somehow, she couldn't just say that. She couldn't tell anyone it was someone else's ideas that got her the producer job.

First, she needed to prove herself. She needed to come up with some great thoughts for the show on her own. Then she'd tell the class that she had a little help with the first few.

After class Stephanie decided to walk home—slowly—to think things over. "See you later, guys," she called to Darcy and Allie as they headed for the bus stop.

"You're not coming with us?" Darcy asked.

"I've got a ton of things to think over as producer," Stephanie said. "And I'm going to work on them right now."

Alone on the street, Stephanie flipped through her pad and sighed. Fresh new ideas? A different kind of sportscast? The only thing Stephanie could picture was a reporter wearing a blazer, standing in front of a field, interviewing a player. Boring!

She didn't have a clue what to do with fashion or anything else—at least not anything exciting. That was just what everyone expected her to come up with . . . something exciting. Something different.

Stephanie flipped her notepad closed. There was only one way she could come up with anything that was really hip, she realized.

She had to talk to Maura.

CHAPTER

8

◆ ◂ ◾ ◆

As soon as she got home, Stephanie made a beeline for the telephone desk in the living room. She reached for the San Francisco phone book to look up Maura's number.

She stopped, her hand holding the phone book in midair. She didn't need to look up the number, she realized. She *remembered* it. She picked up the receiver and punched in the number from memory.

Wow! I can't believe Maura's number is still in my head, Stephanie thought.

It was as though Maura was *always* a part of her life.

Maybe she is, Stephanie realized with surprise.

On the other end, Stephanie heard the phone ring. Please let Maura be home, she thought. I need some ideas—and quick!

"Hello?"

"Maura! I'm *so* glad you're there." Stephanie almost cheered.

"Who is this?" Maura asked.

"It's *Stephanie*," she responded.

Then she realized she couldn't expect Maura to recognize her voice after all this time. She tried to hide her embarrassment. "Uh—Stephanie *Tanner*?"

"Oh." Maura sounded surprised. Then her voice warmed. "Hi, Steph."

"Well, I thought I'd call to see how you were doing. It was fun talking to you the other day." She meant it, she realized. She really did enjoy talking to Maura.

"Yeah, it was nice," Maura agreed. "How's that video project coming along?"

"Pretty good," Stephanie told her. "I'm the producer now, and there's so much to decide. We have to come up with—"

"Stephanie!" Michelle stormed into the living room, interrupting Stephanie's conversation.

"Where have you been?" Michelle asked. Don't you remember we have to go shopping for camp? You told Dad you'd take me today!"

Stephanie gulped. She couldn't believe she had totally forgotten. She couldn't tell that to Michelle. Michelle might let it slip to Danny. Then Danny would think Stephanie was being irresponsible. That would mean bye-bye credit card.

"Steph, are you still there?" Maura asked.

57

"I'm here," she said. "Could you hold on a sec?"

Stephanie turned to Michelle. She covered the phone. "We'll go to the sporting goods store right now," she promised.

"Hey, Maura," she said, taking her hand off the receiver. "I just had an idea. I have to take Michelle shopping for summer camp. Do you want to come? We're going to The Sporting Life."

Stephanie crossed her fingers and waited for Maura's reply. If Maura said yes, Stephanie could accomplish two things at once, taking Michelle shopping *and* working on *Scribe TV*.

"The Sporting Life? Is that at the mall?" Maura asked.

"Uh-uh," Stephanie said, holding her breath.

"Sure," Maura agreed. "I'll meet you there!"

At the mall, Michelle tugged Stephanie quickly down the hall to The Sporting Life. Maura was waiting outside the store. She wore a flowered dress with glass buttons and big, thick shoulder pads. It was the kind of old-fashioned dress that Stephanie had seen in some of the black and white movies her father liked.

Stephanie glanced at her own jeans and sneakers and pictured herself standing next to Maura. They'd look like something from a science-fiction time warp: The forties meets the nineties in a mall. Okay, so we look a bit weird together, Stephanie told herself. But what difference does that make?

She grinned and waved. "Hi, Maura!"

"Hi, Maura!" Michelle chimed in. "Are you and Steph friends again?"

Stephanie felt her face grow hot with embarrassment. "Come on, you two," she said, not giving Maura a chance to answer. "We've got shopping to do."

Inside, Maura looked amused by the racks of brightly colored hiking shorts, rain jackets, and Rollerblading gear.

"I love vintage clothing, so I always shop at the secondhand stores," Maura told Stephanie. "Being in a place like this is . . . different."

"I need a flashlight, a mess kit, a sleeping bag, a compass, bug repellent, hiking socks—" Michelle broke in.

"Did you memorize the whole list?" Stephanie asked, amazed.

"Only the important stuff," Michelle assured her.

"Well, why don't you start in the camping supplies aisle," Stephanie directed. "I'll meet you over there."

"No problem!" Michelle tore off down the camping supplies aisle.

Stephanie turned to Maura. "So, like I was saying on the phone, we've handed out staff assignments. Not much else has been done. We have to come up with new ways to do the news. You know, to make it really cool . . . like that set you suggested."

"Well," Maura said thoughtfully. "Do you know what you'll be covering yet?"

"School news, athletic events, anything that's of interest to the kids at John Muir." Stephanie checked her notepad. "There's a swim meet next week. I gave Darcy the assignment. But I'm not sure how we can handle it. You know, to make it really stand out."

Maura walked over to the aisle where the store sold swimming gear. She held up a pair of goggles and some fins and smiled. "I know what you can do," she said. "Darcy could wear swim goggles to the meet, like she's an actual participant. And you could do that with all the sports. If Darcy's covering a baseball game, she could wear a baseball uniform."

Stephanie nodded. "That's a different way to do the sports, all right."

"Wait," Maura went on, really getting into it. "You could superimpose Darcy's face into the action. It would be like she's one of the players, giving a blow-by-blow description."

"I wonder if we could do that in editing," Stephanie said. "I'll have to ask Ms. Blith, but it's a great idea, and then we could. . . ."

Stephanie's voice trailed off as she heard shouts coming from the other end of the store. There was some commotion going on. Some kind of trouble.

She craned her neck, looking all around. Michelle was nowhere to be seen.

"Uh-oh," she said to Maura. "I have a funny feeling about this."

Stephanie hurried toward the source of the noise. It was coming from the camping department!

A crowd was gathered around a tent set up in the middle of the floor. The tent shook wildly. Someone was pounding on it from inside.

"Let me out!" shouted a voice. "Get me out of here!"

"Oh, no," Stephanie groaned. "It's Michelle!"

"Excuse me, excuse me." Stephanie made her way through the crowd. "Michelle!" she called. "What happened?"

"I'm stuck," Michelle cried. "The zipper won't unzip."

"It's okay, Michelle," Maura said in a soothing voice. "We'll get you out of there."

A short, red-faced man with a thick mustache pushed his way through the crowd. "Who's responsible for the child in that tent?" he demanded.

"I am," Stephanie said with a gulp. "She's my sister."

"You told her to go inside there?"

"No, of course not," Stephanie said. "She—"

"Get me out of here," Michelle wailed.

"We are. Just be patient," Stephanie called back.

"I can't. I'm scared!" Michelle said.

61

Angrily, the manager began pulling on the zipper.

Inside the tent, Michelle began reading a tag aloud. " 'Constructed of light, breathable fabric' . . . I don't think it's breathing so well. It's hot in here," she said loudly.

People in the store started to laugh. The manager looked even angrier. He gave the zipper a hard yank, and it tore away from the fabric with a loud *scritching* sound.

Oh, great! Stephanie thought. She had a very bad feeling about all of this.

Michelle stepped through the hole in the tent, smiling. "Thanks," she said.

"You just bought yourself a tent, young lady," the manager snapped.

"Wait a minute," Stephanie said. "We don't need a tent. We can't buy that."

"You don't have a choice," the man told her. "That zipper was just fine before your sister got inside. You broke it, you buy it."

"It's okay, Steph. I could probably use a tent at camp," Michelle said.

"Good," the manager said with a smile. He flipped over the price tag. "That'll be three hundred forty-one dollars and ninety-nine cents."

What—$341.99? Stephanie felt sick to her stomach. How could the tent be so expensive? It wasn't even on Michelle's list.

"How are you going to pay for that?" Maura whispered.

"My dad," Stephanie whimpered. "He's letting me use his credit card."

"Boy, is he going to be sorry," Michelle said.

"No, he won't," Stephanie insisted. "I'll find a way to pay him back. *If* I can figure out how to explain it to him in the first place."

Once again Stephanie found herself totally out of ideas. And this time even Maura couldn't help her.

CHAPTER
9

◆ ◀ ◼ ◆

Don't think about it, Stephanie told herself as she lay in bed awake all that night. *Don't think about the tent and the money you owe.*

The credit card bill probably wouldn't come for another month, she figured. Which still gave her plenty of time to prove to Danny that she was responsible. Also she could work over the summer, Stephanie promised herself. Baby-sitting, odd jobs, whatever it took to pay back the money. For now, though, she'd just keep the whole thing quiet—and stash the tent in a closet.

"Michelle," Stephanie said as they lay under the covers that night. "You won't tell Dad, will you?"

"About what?" Michelle asked sleepily.

"About the tent," Stephanie said.

"He's going to find out sooner or later," Michelle pointed out.

"But if it's later," Stephanie said, "I'll have more of a chance to figure out how I'm going to pay for it."

Michelle turned over and faced the wall. "Okay," she said. "But it's not really our fault, anyway. That zipper shouldn't have gotten stuck. And it's that mean manager who tore the tent. Not us."

"Tell that to Dad," Stephanie said.

"Well, I would," Michelle said, "only you just told me not to—"

"All right, all right," Stephanie said. "I'll handle it. I promise. Just go to sleep."

Stephanie was in a much better mood the next afternoon. She took the bus home with Allie and Darcy and thought about her day.

Maura's sports-reporting idea was a hit at the video-journalism class. Plus, they were really moving ahead on the newscast. The team worked out schedules and Stephanie gave out deadlines.

Most of the stories were pretty standard stuff, Stephanie knew. School sports, human interest stories. Not much different from what they covered in *The Scribe*. The difference would be in the angle. The way they *told* the story.

The set was coming together, too. Eric brought in lots of funky posters, and they found an old purple velvet couch in the teachers' lounge they could use.

"Tell you what," Allie suggested. "Let's not go home yet. There's a street fair in the Marina. Why don't we stop by and see what's going on? It's Friday and we deserve the afternoon off."

"Sounds good to me," Darcy said. "I read about it in the *Chronicle*."

Stephanie debated a moment. I really want to go, but I probably shouldn't. I have about a zillion name tags to sew on for Michelle.

But then—she had a fabulous thought. "Did you say you read about it in the *Chronicle*?" she asked Darcy.

"Yup. It was on the front page," her friend answered.

"Well, if it's in the *news*paper, it must be news," Stephanie observed. "I think that we may have a journalistic responsibility to check this fair out."

Darcy grinned. "A journalistic responsibility? Definitely."

Half an hour later the three girls got off the city bus they'd taken to the Marina district. Booths and stands lined the streets, and crowds spilled onto the grassy waterfront. Banners and balloons flew from the boats that were docked in the bay. A band played on a stage off to one side.

"So what do you think?" Allie asked Stephanie. "How would you handle this type of thing for

Scribe TV? I'm sure you have plenty of great ideas."

Stephanie hesitated. She never really meant to give the impression that all the ideas she suggested were hers. In class she just burst out with them, eager to tell everyone. But now it was just her and Darcy and Allie. Maybe now she should start explaining that the ideas were Maura's. And who better to start with than her two best friends?

"Listen," Stephanie said. "There's something I've been meaning to tell you. All those ideas? Well, they were—"

"Hey, look!" Darcy nudged Stephanie and pointed down the street. Maura Potter stood near a stand whose sign read: PAST TIMES BOUTIQUE: VINTAGE FINDS. Maura stood with her side to a wood-framed mirror, squinting at her reflection. She had a beaded shawl around her shoulders and a wide-brimmed straw hat on her head.

Allie shook her head in disbelief. "You'd think she was getting dressed up for a costume party. But that's exactly the kind of stuff she wears to school. *What* is she thinking?"

Stephanie knew she ought to stick up for Maura. "Maybe Maura likes vintage clothing," she said to her friends. "Is that so terrible?"

"No," Darcy answered. "But it is a little weird."

"Maybe what you really mean is different," Stephanie said carefully. "I mean, maybe we're all a little weird—"

"Not *that* weird," Darcy pointed out. "The way Maura dresses, she might be from the moon."

"Well, I think it's kind of cool," Stephanie said.

"Cool?" Allie echoed. "Freaky is more like it."

"Hey, come on, Allie," Stephanie said. "Don't you remember all the fun we used to have with Maura? Those picnics and sleepovers? And, Darcy, I know you'd have been friends with her, too."

"What was she like back in elementary school?" Darcy asked, curious.

"Well, she was awfully fun to be with," Allie admitted. "Kind of original. Unique. Even back then."

"I've heard her talking to teachers," Darcy said. "And she always has this unique way of looking at things."

Stephanie felt herself begin to relax. Darcy and Allie *would* be fine with Maura, she thought. Maybe she could even invite them all over to her house. . . .

"She always had great ideas for different things to do when we were younger," Allie added.

Stephanie saw her chance. "Maura had the best ideas," she said, "and she still does. She—"

Stephanie was just about to get into the Maura/ *Scribe TV* story, when Darcy's dark eyes widened. "Uh-oh. Here comes trouble," she murmured.

Stephanie's heart sank as she saw Tiffany strolling down the street with Rene Salter, the head of the Flamingoes. Tiffany and Rene stared straight at Maura. And Maura was trying on her worst out-fit yet—a bright, short-sleeved Hawaiian shirt with a dark burgundy lace skirt.

"Maura," Rene said loudly, "did you put that outfit together all by yourself? It's amazing. Amazingly awful!"

"I wish I had the video camera here," Tiffany chimed in. "You'd be perfect for our first fashion feature on *Scribe TV*—what *not* to wear. Ever!"

Stephanie felt terrible as she saw Maura's face turn bright red.

"I-I wasn't going to wear them together," Maura stammered.

"But you should," Rene said. "It's really very memorable. I know I'll remember it for the rest of my life." She turned to Tiffany, laughing. "What is wrong with that girl?" she said even more loudly. "Doesn't she know how weird she is?"

Poor Maura! Stephanie thought. No matter what her taste in clothing, she didn't deserve to be shredded by the Flamingoes.

The woman who ran the Past Times stand suddenly stepped out of the booth, placing herself between Maura and the Flamingoes. Tall and slender, the woman wore a long, dark green velvet skirt and an ivory lace blouse. She had glossy, waist-length blue-black hair, very tan skin, and eyes that were nearly black. Stephanie thought she was stunning.

"And what gives you the right to put anyone

else down?" the woman asked Rene. "I don't see anything original or even remotely interesting in the way *you* dress."

Rene opened her mouth and closed it again silently.

"All right! Tell her!" Darcy whispered to her friends.

The woman turned to Tiffany. "And what are you, her sidekick? You two in a contest to see which one can be meaner?"

Stephanie wondered if the woman was making things even worse for Maura. Then she realized that the Hawaiian shirt and lace skirt were hanging neatly on a hanger by the mirror. Maura was gone, swallowed up by the crowds.

She turned to see the two Flamingoes walking swiftly away from the clothing booth, their faces flushed with embarrassment.

"Wow," Allie said in an awed voice. "Someone finally gave the Flamingoes what they deserve. That woman is fierce!"

"Yeah," Darcy agreed. "I bet that's one story Tiffany won't be repeating."

"Well, not that part of it, anyway," Stephanie said in a worried voice. She was pretty sure that Tiffany, who was a major gossip, would find something to tell the whole school. "I just hope that now Rene doesn't decide to really go after Maura."

"I hope not," Darcy said. "But if she does, it won't last."

"Right," Allie said. "It's only a matter of time before Rene finds someone new to pick on."

Stephanie wanted her friends to be as mad as she felt on Maura's behalf.

Except that, even though she was angry and upset for Maura, she felt like a hypocrite. Something kept nagging at the back of her brain, a feeling of relief that no one knew where her best *Scribe TV* ideas came from.

Even worse, she felt glad that she decided to keep her meetings with Maura a secret. And that the Flamingoes had never seen the two of them hanging out.

If they did, it could just as easily have been Stephanie the Flamingoes were making fun of. She could be made just as much of a social outcast as Maura was.

Stephanie and her two friends slowly walked toward the waterfront. Sailboats glided beneath the Golden Gate Bridge, and windsurfers traced patterns on the bay. Stephanie settled down on an open patch of grass to watch them. Darcy and Allie walked off to find a cookie stand.

Stephanie wondered, *If I'm helping to make Maura a social outcast by not admitting to be friends with her, am I any better than the Flamingoes?*

Stephanie stared out at the water with a troubled sigh. She barely looked up when Darcy and Allie returned.

Darcy sat down beside her and offered Stephanie

an oatmeal raisin cookie. "What's wrong?" Darcy asked.

"Ever notice how our whole school is caught up in cliques?" Stephanie asked.

"You can't miss the Flamingoes," Allie said. "They're the biggest, pinkest clique of all."

"It's not just them," Stephanie said. "*The Scribe* staff is kind of a little clique of its own. And so are the basketball and baseball teams and the cheerleaders. And even the three of us are a clique. It's like everyone in the school has some exclusive little group they belong to. Everyone except Maura."

"That must be really hard on her," Darcy said.

"Maybe not," Allie disagreed. "Most of the time it seems like Maura doesn't even notice anyone else. It's like she's lost in her own dream world or something. Maybe she doesn't want to hang out with any of us."

"We'll never find out if we don't talk to her," Stephanie said.

"Steph, you seem really worried about Maura. Why?" Darcy asked.

Stephanie hesitated. But she still couldn't bring herself to tell them that not only was Maura helping her with ideas, she considered Maura a friend.

"I just hate to see the Flamingoes attack anyone," Stephanie finally said. "And I'm beginning to think that if the Flamingoes *don't* like someone, then you can bet that person is probably really nice and interesting."

Allie grinned. "Reverse snobbery."

"Maybe," Stephanie admitted. "And it bugs me that Tiffany was using her position as fashion reporter for *Scribe TV* to put Maura down."

"You did tell her she'd be the ultimate word on fashion," Darcy reminded her.

Stephanie winced. "I've created a monster."

"Nope, you just encouraged one," Allie said cheerfully.

"Great," Stephanie moaned. "That makes me feel a lot better."

She was not feeling good about herself. She'd let down a friend. And she knew she was still a long way from really standing up for her.

CHAPTER
10

◆ ◀ ◖ ◆

The next Monday after school Stephanie stood in the cafeteria, scanning a list of items on her clipboard. She looked up as Eric carried more posters and props onto the *Scribe TV* set—a big crocheted throw for the couch, a lava lamp, and an old armchair. Stephanie added the items to her list.

"Let's see," she said. "We've got that big comfy couch. The chair—that's good for interviews. An old standing lamp with a fringed shade. And these posters."

She thumbed through the old movie posters. One pictured gangsters playing cards, another a happy family singing around a piano, and the third, people running from a monstrous gorilla.

"These are great," she said.

She stared in disbelief as Eric dragged in one

more prop: a plaster of Paris moosehead. "That's it!" Stephanie said, grinning. "We have everything we need!"

Allie handed Stephanie a stack of scripts. "These are for the prerecorded segments," she said. "Have a look."

Stephanie read through them and felt a thrill of satisfaction. "Everyone is doing a great job," she said.

"Absolutely," Ms. Blith agreed. "Let's just keep in mind that in two short weeks we're on the air."

And the responsibility to make sure we're ready is mine, Stephanie added silently.

"Let's run through the topics we'll be covering in our first newscast," she said out loud.

"I've divided the stories into categories," Allie said. She brought over a computer printout.

Stephanie began to transfer the information to a blackboard for everyone to see.

"School news," Stephanie said, writing down the first heading. "We have new fire alarms being put in. The old ones keep going off for no reason. And two teachers are getting married. Mr. Jennings and Ms. Tipton."

"Who are they marrying?" Darcy asked.

"Each other, silly," Tiffany snipped. "Can't you tell by the way they're always gazing at each other in the cafeteria? I've even seen them at the mall, buying house stuff." She rolled her eyes. "Not the best taste in linens."

"Okay," Stephanie said. "We'll use the marriage piece because it's interesting. But we're not going to do it in a gossipy way. Shawna, would you cover that story?"

"No problem," Shawna said.

"Now on to local news," Stephanie said, scribbling that category on the chalkboard. "There's a boat race in the Bay. And a new just-for-teens store opening in the mall."

"Sporting events," Darcy read over Stephanie's shoulder. "That comes next." Stephanie added the school swim meet to the list.

"Weather," Quentin piped up. "I'm downloading daily reports and weather maps from the National Weather Service. I can have up-to-the-minute data."

"What about late-breaking stories?" Sue asked. "We need to include anything newsworthy that comes up, too."

Stephanie blushed. How could she forget? They were going live on the air. They'd be able to include items at the last minute, as soon as they happened. "Of course," she said quickly. She squeezed in "latest news," in the corner of the blackboard.

"Good work," Ms. Blith told the class. "The show's content is really coming together."

"But we still need a *Scribe TV* take on these things," Gia said. "Something—maybe a visual or theme music—something totally cool that makes the show instantly identifiable as *Scribe TV*."

Everyone turned to Stephanie.

She took a deep breath. If she could come up with some really fresh ideas—well, maybe even just one—then she'd feel better about using Maura's. Maybe she could even come clean and tell the class that the other ideas had come from Maura. . . .

Stephanie waited a moment, hoping inspiration would hit. Seconds ticked by. Tiffany tapped her foot. Gia began to doodle.

"I—uh—" Stephanie began. Everyone looked up at her expectantly. Stephanie cleared her throat.

"Okay," she began. "Here's what I think. . . ."

She froze, unable to finish the sentence. Instead, she stared at Tiffany. The Flamingo stared back at her, as if to say, Go ahead. Give us one of your totally boring, un-hip ideas.

"You know," Josh said thoughtfully, "Gia and I just started to work with the editing machine. We don't even know what that thing is capable of doing yet. There may be all kinds of nifty special effects and stuff we could use. Why don't you give us another day or so to figure it out?"

"That's a great idea," Stephanie said. She thought she was about to collapse with relief. "Just keep me up-to-date on it, okay?"

"Sure thing," Josh said with a nod.

Stephanie relaxed a little and spent the rest of the meeting organizing the shooting schedule.

"Okay, people," she wrapped up. "Let's meet again tomorrow."

"We'll discuss the special *Scribe TV* look then, right?" Gia asked.

"Right." Stephanie smiled. "I can't wait."

Stephanie went straight from the video meeting to the Y where Maura took her poetry class.

She asked at the information desk and was relieved to hear that the class was still in session. Stephanie followed directions to a lecture hall at the end of the building.

The door was open. Stephanie peered in. There were only five people in the room. An older man, whom Stephanie guessed was the teacher, and four students. All the other students were older, too, Stephanie noticed.

Maura stood at the front of the room at a little podium. She wasn't looking out at the audience, but at the piece of paper that rested on the podium. She read aloud in her soft voice,

". . . *A silver moon rises over the rim of the
mountains
And I set out on my journey home.*"

Maura looked up and the other students applauded. With a shy smile she left the podium and took a seat.

"That was lovely, Maura," the teacher said.

"Nice, strong imagery, especially in your opening verse."

Stephanie waited while the teacher and the other students critiqued Maura's poem. All of them really liked it. The teacher even said she was one of the most talented young poets he'd heard. Stephanie couldn't help but be impressed. In John Muir Middle School, people considered Maura an outcast. Here, she shone.

Stephanie waited while the teacher gave an assignment for their next class, and everyone gathered their books and packs.

She met Maura at the door.

"Hi," Stephanie said.

Maura looked startled to see her. "Hi," she said. "How long have you been here?"

"Not long," Stephanie told her. "I heard only the last two lines of your poem. I wish I'd heard the whole thing."

Maura blushed. "It was just a short one. Maybe I'll show it to you someday."

"I'd really like that," Stephanie said. "Um—our video class just got out, so I was wondering if you wanted to ride the bus home together."

"Sure," Maura said. "That would be great."

The two girls walked toward the bus stop. Today Maura was dressed in black jeans, a white shirt, and an old silk brocade vest with a pattern of gold and crimson swirls. No one else in John Muir dressed that way, but Stephanie thought it looked great. It was definitely more sophisticated and interesting than the Flamingoes' constant pink. Stephanie was starting to think of them as the Bubblegum Brigade. Either that, or walking bottles of calamine lotion.

The bus was nowhere in sight, so the two girls sat down on the bench to wait.

"How's Michelle doing?" Maura asked. "Ready for camp?"

"Almost," Stephanie said. "I'm taking her shopping at The Good-Buy Mart on our half day. She needs a lot of odds and ends for camp, and I figure that's the best place to get them."

Stephanie hesitated, wanting Maura to offer to come along. When Maura didn't speak up, Stephanie said, "It would be nice to have some company."

"I'd love to come," Maura said shyly.

"Great!" Stephanie said. "So, I've been wanting to ask you something . . . do you remember why we stopped being friends? I don't."

"It was in fifth grade," Maura said. "You and Allie wanted to be friends with that girl who moved here from Seattle."

"Teresa Raimo," Stephanie said, remembering. "Her family moved to Florida at the end of sixth grade."

"I don't know what happened with Teresa," Maura said. "All I remember is you two started being friends with her and stopped being friends with me."

Stephanie remembered. Teresa Raimo had seemed very cool at the time. She'd told Stephanie and Allie that Maura Potter had "the un-cool disease." Now Stephanie knew that "the un-cool disease" was something Teresa made up. But at the time, Teresa had convinced both Stephanie and Allie that they would catch it from Maura. So they stopped hanging out with her.

Stephanie's eyes widened as she realized: She was still acting as though Maura had some contagious "un-cool disease."

"Teresa was a moron," Stephanie said. "And Allie and I didn't act all that much more intelligent. I'm sorry."

Maura shrugged. "It happens. Kids are weird."

Stephanie thought of what had happened at the street fair the other day. "Worse than weird," she said. "Cruel."

Maura nodded. "I'm just not the kind who's going to fit in," she said. "I understand that, and I'm okay with it. I mean, the last thing on earth I'd want to do is walk around dressed in pink every day. Talk about boring . . ."

Stephanie laughed. "I know what you mean."

"There's the bus," Maura said.

It occurred to Stephanie that this would be a good time to ask Maura to brainstorm with her about the *Scribe TV* look, but for once she didn't want to. This time she just wanted to be friends with Maura.

Stephanie and Maura boarded the bus together. Could I really be her friend? Stephanie asked herself. She wanted to. She genuinely liked Maura. Also, she hated the way the Flamingoes acted. She knew she didn't want to be anything like them. On the other hand, Stephanie still didn't know if she had the courage to be friends openly with someone whom the whole school shunned.

This is about courage, Stephanie realized. Courage to be exactly who you are, no matter what anyone else thinks. Maura has more of that kind of courage than just about anyone in John Muir. The question is, do I?

CHAPTER
11

♦ ◄ ◆ ♦

"Yes, Dad." Stephanie held the phone against her ear. "Okay, Dad." She listened for another moment, then said. "I know, Dad. I will, Dad."

"I know you hear me. But I'm not sure you're really listening, honey," Danny told her.

Her father was calling from Calgary, Canada, checking to see how everything was going.

"It's not that I don't trust you," he said. "I know you're doing your best. But you've got a lot to deal with—Michelle and the video project, not to mention your regular schoolwork. And I can't help out. The next two weeks are really crazy for Becky and me. We'll be flying all over the country."

"Really, Dad," Stephanie assured him. "Everything's fine. School's almost over, so there's not too much work. The video project is under control.

And I'm taking Michelle to The Good-Buy Mart tomorrow afternoon. It's a half day at school. We'll call when we get back to tell you exactly what we bought."

"Are you sure?" her father asked.

"Positive," Stephanie told him. "I can handle everything."

"Okay, Steph," Danny said, sounding relieved. "I appreciate all the work you're doing. You're really being a big help."

If you only knew, Stephanie thought as she hung up the phone. She'd taken Michelle shopping once and wound up with a very expensive ripped tent. They hadn't even started to pack. And Danny would be home in two weeks.

Stephanie resolved that she really would be more responsible. She went up to her room and threaded the needle. Then she picked up a pair of shorts from the huge pile of Michelle's clothing and began sewing on name tags.

Stephanie and Michelle got to The Good-Buy Mart at 1:55. Stephanie rushed Michelle to get there quickly. She couldn't wait to see Maura! Josh and Gia had not been able to come up with a cool visual effect from the editing machine.

Scribe TV was once again depending on Stephanie to give them a fresh take on things. And *Stephanie* still didn't have a clue as to what that take would be.

Maybe, Steph hoped, Maura would.

Stephanie sat down on the wooden bench outside the store. "We're five minutes early," she said, checking her watch.

"Are we meeting Maura?" Michelle asked.

"Yup. She'll be here at two," Stephanie said. She looked at her sister curiously. "Michelle, what do *you* think of Maura?"

"I like her," Michelle answered.

"Why?" Stephanie wanted to know.

"Because she's nice," Michelle said. "And she's totally cool."

Stephanie thought about it. Michelle had nothing to do with the cliques at John Muir. She didn't know Maura was considered weird there. So she just saw her as she was—totally cool.

"There she is now." Michelle pointed out the door.

Maura was walking toward them. She was wearing an ankle-length pale yellow dress with a long string of amber beads.

"She looks like something out of a movie," Michelle said with awe.

"She does," Stephanie agreed. "Hi," she called out.

"Hi, Steph. Hi, Michelle," Maura said. She smiled at Michelle. "Ready to shop till you drop?"

"Definitely," Michelle said.

Which gave Stephanie an idea. "I need to talk to Maura," she told her sister. "If I give you the

85

list of the stuff you need, do you think you could start shopping on your own?"

Michelle glared at Stephanie as if she were nuts. "Of course I can," she said.

"Thanks," Stephanie said. "We'll be right here, outside the store." She handed her sister the list that Danny had given her. "You need a travel toothbrush, toothpaste, shampoo, sunscreen, a laundry bag, and, well . . . you can read the rest yourself. And here's some money. Meet me back here in twenty minutes."

"No problem." Michelle waved cheerfully, then went into the store and set off down an aisle. Stephanie turned to Maura. "Is it okay if we just sit here and talk?"

"Sure. That sounds nice. So, how's the rest of your family?" Maura began. "I haven't seen any of them for so long."

Stephanie filled Maura in on her dad, and D.J., and everyone else. Somehow, she thought, I've got to get the subject back to *Scribe TV.*

"So that's all the family news," she said. "And speaking of news—your ideas have been so great for our news show."

Maura smiled. "That's good to know. Have you come up with anything else?"

Stephanie shook her head. "I wish! Only a few more days now, and we'll begin shooting. We still don't have a clue what to do with the weather segment to make it really stand out. And we're still looking for some kind of *Scribe TV* visual or music clip. Something that will make our newscasts instantly identifiable."

"Let's start with the weather," Maura said thoughtfully. She gazed around. Her eyes came to rest on a sign in the window. It was a cardboard cutout of a beach scene. The words on the sign read GET READY FOR SUMMER! BEAT THE HEAT!

Maura snapped her fingers. "I've got it! How about a Hot Spot break in the middle of the weather report? *Scribe TV* can give tips for the hottest new in places to go. Maybe you can have that wavy look on-screen. You know, to make it seem really hot and melting."

"How do you do that?" Stephanie asked, amazed. "You're incredible!"

Maura shrugged. "I guess I just like brainstorming. It's fun to spark ideas in each other. So what else do you need?"

"I'm not sure exactly," Stephanie said. "But it would be great to have some kind of logo or image or something—so that viewers always know they're watching *Scribe TV.*"

"And as for the visual—" Maura reached down into her big embroidered bag and drew out a pad and a pencil. "I can't draw," she said apologetically, "but what if you played with the image of a scribe?"

"What do you mean?" Stephanie asked.

"Well, a scribe is someone who writes things

down," Maura said. "So what if you had stick-figure drawings or a cartoon that would keep changing and show scribes through the ages? You could have a prehistoric scribe carving a stone tablet, and a medieval guy with a quill and parchment."

"And then someone at a typewriter. And a modern kid at a computer!" Stephanie said, catching on to the idea.

Maura drew a few rough sketches that made Stephanie smile.

"Someone writing in the dirt with a stick, a teacher at a blackboard, even," Maura said. "You just have to keep showing changing images of someone writing, taking it all down."

"We could have the scribe in the upper corner of the screen," Stephanie said. "Like a TV logo."

"Exactly!" Maura said. "It doesn't have to be complicated. It's probably better if it's cartoonlike and kind of funny."

Stephanie looked at Maura. "You know, I really like working with everyone on the *Scribe TV* staff, but I wish you were one of them. Your ideas are the best!"

Maura smiled. "Well, we are sort of working together, anyway. You know, I can make a list of different scribe images to use and give it to you in school. Do you want to have lunch? We can sit together in the cafeteria."

Stephanie felt herself panicking. She was determined to be Maura's friend. Yet, somehow she imagined that being friends with Maura was something that would happen gradually. Over the summer. When they could meet outside of school.

Despite her best intentions, Stephanie simply wasn't ready to sit in the middle of the John Muir cafeteria with Maura Potter. She just couldn't handle the fallout right now—not with so many other things going on in her life.

Darcy and Allie might understand about her hanging out with Maura. But everyone else would make her life miserable. What could she say?

"Stephanie! I'm finished!" She turned at the voice.

Stephanie breathed a sigh of relief as Michelle rushed over with two huge plastic shopping bags. Whew! Saved by her sister!

This was her chance to make a quick escape without having to answer Maura's invitation. She grabbed her sister by the arm and pulled her toward the bus stop.

"I'm sorry, but we've got to go home now," she explained to Maura. "Michelle needs a snack. You know how little kids get if they don't eat for a while."

"Hey!" Michelle cried. "I'm not a baby!"

"Shhh!" Stephanie hissed. "Let's just go."

"Byeeee!" Michelle bellowed to Maura as Stephanie pulled her away.

"I'll talk to you later," Stephanie called as they rushed down the street. "Thanks for all your help!"

Back at the house, Stephanie turned on the TV and began channel-surfing.

She wanted to check out the music video stations and the twenty-four-hour news station to see if they sparked any ideas in her head.

She was still more than a little worried—and more than a little guilty—about the fact that her best ideas always seemed to be Maura's. Maybe this would give her some inspiration of her own.

"What should we do now?" Michelle asked. She squeezed next to Stephanie on the couch.

"What do you mean?" Stephanie looked at Michelle. "We did major shopping. I think that's enough for today. Besides, I need to work on *Scribe TV*."

"What about my snack?" Michelle asked.

"You said it yourself—you're not a baby. Fix it yourself if you want it," Stephanie told her.

"Well, at least help me unpack this stuff." Michelle waved at the bags from The Good-Buy Mart in Stephanie's face.

"Not now, Michelle. We can do it later." Didn't little sisters ever understand? Steph needed to watch these shows, not put away Q-tips.

Stephanie concentrated on the screen. A reporter

stood in front of a flower store, talking about allergies. Was there a story there for *Scribe TV*?

"Is it okay to call Dad?" Michelle asked.

"Do whatever you want," Stephanie told her, not paying attention. *Allergies*, she scribbled on her notepad. *Look into.*

Michelle stepped in front of the TV set. Stephanie craned her neck to look around her. Then Michelle reached for the phone, still blocking the screen.

"Michelle," Stephanie yelled.

"All right! All right!" Michelle shouted back. She stepped out of the way of the screen and dialed the phone.

The news had moved onto a pets segment. That could be interesting. "Pets," she wrote. *Lots of kids in John Muir have them. Interviews? Advice?*

"Dad?" Michelle said into the phone. "It's me."

She paused a moment, then said, "Well—Stephanie and I are *sort of* getting everything done. We just got back from the Good-Buy Mart."

Michelle began pulling out items from the bags. "Let's see. I got some really cool hair clips. They're shaped like caterpillars and butterflies. Two water guns, just in case one of them gets broken. A pack of balloons and these bracelets that glow in the dark. Gum, candy, corn chips, and cheese popcorn. This is the best—a Pretty Princess Make-Yourself-Up Kit!"

What? Stephanie jumped up from the couch.

Now Michelle had all her attention. She looked at the play makeup and everything else Michelle had bought, openmouthed. What happened to the sunscreen and toothpaste?

Michelle held the phone away from her ear. Stephanie heard Danny's voice shouting from the other end. "Michelle, put your sister on the phone!"

Stephanie winced. She took the telephone. How was she going to explain this one? She couldn't tell her father she'd let Michelle loose in the store with a ton of money. Could she?

No, she decided. He'd tell her that she was irresponsible and immature. In short, definitely not credit card material.

"Hi, Dad," Stephanie said cheerfully. "How's the trip going? How's the Grand Canyon?"

"It's great, Steph. But what's going on there? Why did you let Michelle buy all that junk?"

"I did it on purpose," Stephanie told him, thinking quickly. "It was just my way of uh . . . uh . . . teaching Michelle responsibility. We're going back to the store right now to return everything and buy what she really needs."

"Stephanie—do you really expect me to believe—" Danny's tone was suspicious.

"Honest, we were just on our way back to the store," Stephanie interrupted. "So we'll call you tomorrow, okay?"

"Okay—" Danny agreed reluctantly. "Just make sure that your sister gets what she really needs."

"Don't worry about anything," Stephanie said. "I've got it all under control." She hung up the phone.

Or, at least, I'd better get it all under control—right now!

CHAPTER
12

◆ ◂   ◗   ◆

Okay, now, let's see. Stephanie stretched out on her bed. She ran her eyes over her schedule for the past week, trying to see if she'd missed any tasks she'd assigned herself.

The video project was picking up steam, and she'd met with Maura the past couple of days to get more ideas.

Stephanie had chosen the places where they'd met so she wouldn't have to worry about running into John Muir kids.

Stephanie smiled, remembering how they'd smushed into a corner study cubicle at the library. A librarian had had to come over—twice—to tell them to keep it down, they were laughing so hard.

Stephanie smiled again, remembering Larson Park, a toddler playground. It was another place

Stephanie felt sure no one from John Muir would go, so she had met Maura there.

She and Maura had discussed the pet-story idea there, surrounded by screaming two-year-olds running under the sprinklers. It looked like so much fun that she and Maura had finally taken off their shoes and run through the sprinkler, too.

Stephanie yawned, and suddenly realized how tired she felt. No matter what she told her father, getting Michelle ready for camp was a lot of work on top of the video project and school. Stephanie stifled another big yawn. Maybe she could just shut her eyes for a minute. . . .

"Stephanie." Michelle stomped up the steps, then flung open the door to their room. "Do you realize what day it is?"

"Friday. So what?"

"Friday afternoon. This whole week has gone by, and we haven't done any shopping since The Good-Buy Mart. I still need sheets and blankets, and non . . . non . . . nonpleasant foods."

"Nonpleasant foods?" Stephanie grabbed the list. "That's nonperishable foods for camping trips. Foods that won't go bad."

Michelle stamped her foot. "What difference does it make? We haven't gotten any sort of food. I'm going to call Dad and tell him you haven't been taking me shopping."

"Wait," Stephanie pleaded. No way could she let that happen. Not after she had done so much already. "We've got a whole weekend ahead. We have plenty of time," she told Michelle.

"We do?" Michelle said doubtfully.

Stephanie nodded. "You don't leave for camp for two weeks."

"But Dad said we had to have everything done when he gets home," Michelle answered.

"That's not for another week yet," Stephanie said reassuringly to her sister. "Tomorrow we'll do your nonperishable food shopping. And Sunday I'll finish sewing all those name tags in, and then we'll pack everything."

Stephanie jumped out of bed as the phone rang. "Hello?" she answered.

"Hi, Steph. It's Gia."

"What's up?" Stephanie asked.

"I've got some great footage for the fashion segment," Gia told her. "But Josh and I are arguing over how to edit it. So far it's not saying 'hip' like the rest of the pieces do. You're the person with the vision. Give us some ideas."

Stephanie would have screamed if she were sure Gia wouldn't hear her. *More* creative ideas? Stephanie was getting tired of them—even though she hadn't come up with any of them.

"Why don't you two leave that piece alone for a while?" Stephanie instructed Gia. "I'll get back to you with something totally cool. I just need a little time."

Gia agreed, thanked Stephanie, and hung up the phone.

This looks like a job for Maura, Stephanie thought. After all, this whole show has been about her vision, not mine.

But how can I see her when I just promised Michelle I'd spend the whole weekend doing her camp stuff?

"Thanks for meeting me here," Stephanie told Maura. The two girls stood in front of a big natural foods store in the Noe Valley neighborhood. Michelle kicked a pebble nearby. "It's just that I have to finish getting Michelle ready for camp, and I wanted to see you, too."

"No problem," Maura said. "I like shopping with you guys."

Last night Stephanie realized that the only way to accomplish everything she needed to was to combine tasks. She'd have to do two things at once.

She could easily combine taking Michelle shopping and talking to Maura. She'd done it before, at the sporting goods store and The Good-Buy Mart. And now, she figured, she and Maura could brainstorm in the two stores she still had to go to.

Chances were they wouldn't bump into anyone they knew here. The Noe Valley area was a completely different school district. And it had all the stores they needed.

The three girls went into the natural foods store.

This time Stephanie watched closely as Michelle picked out packages of dried fruits and nuts.

Michelle turned to glare at her. "I can do it myself," she said indignantly.

"All right, but this time I'm checking your purchases *before* we pay for them," Stephanie told her sister. She looked around for Maura and found her in the cosmetics aisle.

"I figured if we needed to come up with something for the beauty segment, we should be in the beauty aisle!" Maura said. "Hey! Look at this shampoo!" She held up a bottle. "It's made with honeydew. This one has raspberries. And this one's made from grass."

"Grass?" Stephanie said with a giggle. "You mean I could wash my hair with our backyard?"

"No, silly. But you should think about that for the beauty segment—giving kids tips on how to turn things around the house into beauty treatments!"

Stephanie smiled. As always, she loved Maura's idea.

The two girls roamed the cosmetics aisle, finding more and more exotic products. Stephanie was reading the ingredients for a bar of sesame-seed soap, when she heard Michelle call.

"Stephanie, come look at this!"

Michelle sounded excited. Like she did when she was about to do something. Something Stephanie would regret.

"Michelle!" she cried. "Don't move a muscle! I'll find you!" She raced to the back of the store. She didn't even wait for Maura to follow. "Please don't let her do anything," she begged out loud. "Please!"

Seconds later Stephanie saw a long row of trays stacked one on top of the other. Each one was filled with all sorts of nuts and dried fruits.

"Michelle?" she called a little nervously.

"Over here!"

Stephanie rounded a corner and skidded to a stop. Michelle stood in front of a huge tray of carob-coated walnuts that was in the middle of the stack.

"Don't these look delicious?" Michelle said. She pulled out the tray.

"Stop!" Stephanie cried. "Would you please be careful!"

Michelle wheeled around to face Stephanie, her hand still gripping the tray. The tray slid out farther . . . and farther. . . .

Stephanie groaned as it crashed to the floor with a loud bang. Nuts flew into the air and rolled across the floor.

She stepped closer to her sister to pull her away. But the nuts rolled underfoot. *Crunch!* Stephanie felt herself mashing carob walnuts. She took another step and screeched as her foot slid out from under her and she fell to the ground.

"Stephanie, are you okay?" Maura ran over. *Crunch, crunch, crunch.* More nuts squashed.

Stephanie stood up slowly. She brushed carob off her jeans and glared at Michelle. "I'm fine."

"That's more than I can say for this store." A salesperson stood with hands on hips, scowling. "You realize these walnuts are five ninety-nine a pound?"

Stephanie sighed. Another mess, courtesy of Michelle.

Twenty minutes later Stephanie had finally cleared up the natural foods disaster. Of course, she'd paid for all the mashed nuts—and the stuff Michelle really needed. She'd also swept the floor.

Michelle actually looked upset when they left the store. "I'm sorry, Steph," she said.

"It's okay," Stephanie told her. "Come on."

They crossed the street to the linen store. "Okay, Michelle," Stephanie ordered. "This time I want you to stick to me like glue."

"You got it, Steph." Michelle walked closely behind Stephanie.

Maura laughed as they entered the linen store. "What trouble can Michelle possibly get into here?" she asked.

Stephanie eyed the stacks of pillows, blankets, sheets, and towels. "I'm not sure," she replied. "But if I know my sister, she'll think of something."

"I will not," Michelle said. "I promise."

They walked over to the sheets for single beds and cots.

"I'd like a nice flowery design," Michelle said. "Maybe with daisies or tulips."

"We'll see what they have," Stephanie told her. She turned to Maura. "Now, about that pet segment. We want a real-life feel to it. . . ."

Stephanie spent the next half hour brainstorming ideas with Maura, choosing colors for sheets, and making sure Michelle didn't get into trouble—all at the same time.

Before they knew it, Stephanie and Michelle both had exactly what they needed.

"Well, at least that went smoothly," Stephanie observed. "Let's pay for everything and get out while the getting is good,"

Stephanie grabbed the sheets and towels. She kept an eye on Michelle, and continued talking to Maura while she paid. So much was happening at once that she felt like a juggler trying to keep track of it all.

Finally she said good-bye to Maura and brought Michelle home. Once she got in the door, Stephanie sighed with relief. That last stop hadn't been so terrible. Sure, she felt totally drained. But at least Michelle didn't do anything crazy. And they'd bought everything they needed. Danny would be proud.

Michelle plopped down in front of the TV. Stephanie reached into her back pocket for Danny's credit card so she could leave it on the shelf above the kitchen counter, as she always did.

Stephanie couldn't believe it. She reached in for it a second time. Her pocket was empty.

Empty? What happened to the credit card?

Frantically, Stephanie searched all her pockets. Then she tore through every single bag. She pulled out fruit and nuts and pillows and sheets. But no credit card—anywhere.

Oh, no! Stephanie thought. What if I've really lost it? The consequences were too horrible to consider.

"Michelle, did you see what I did with Dad's credit card?" Stephanie asked. Her voice shook when she spoke.

"The last time I saw it was when you paid for the sheets," Michelle said.

The front door opened and D.J. walked in. She surveyed the mess. "Stephanie, why is there stuff all over the living room?"

"I've been looking for Dad's credit card," Stephanie told her sister. A sob escaped her throat. She felt a tear roll down her cheek. "I think I lost it. What am I going to do?"

"Don't panic," D.J. told her. "I'll help you."

D.J. helped Stephanie look through Michelle's things one last time. But the card was nowhere to be found.

Then she dialed the phone number for the credit

card hotline. She stood by while Stephanie called to report the lost card.

"I had to cancel it," Stephanie groaned as she hung up. "Dad's going to kill me!"

The phone rang. "You answer it," Stephanie told D.J. She felt miserable. "I don't want to talk to anyone."

"Hello?" she heard D.J. say. "Yes, this is the Tanner residence. Yes. Uh-uh. I see. Well, thank you."

D.J. hung up and turned to Stephanie. "That was the linen store. They found the card on the counter."

"Great!" Stephanie brightened. Maybe it wasn't a disaster after all. "We'll call the credit card company and cancel the cancellation."

It was too late. When Stephanie called the credit card company, they said they'd already canceled the card and would have to issue a new one.

Stephanie sighed. *Now Dad will have to find out what happened. And I won't get a credit card till I'm thirty years old!*

CHAPTER

13

Thursday after their last class, Steph, Darcy, and Allie headed straight for the mall. They weren't shopping. They were gearing up to shoot their first Hot Spot.

A new just-for-teens store was opening this month. *Scribe TV* was going to give students a sneak peek at the place. Stephanie looked around. The tiny, narrow store was crammed with posters, books, and gift items. With the *Scribe TV* crew inside, there was almost no room to move.

"Gee, I wonder why they call it The Closet," Eric joked.

Gia smiled. "We're almost ready," she told Stephanie.

"I'll just get Shawna in place to begin filming," Josh said. "Allie, have you got the final script?"

Allie rushed over and handed Shawna two typed pages. Then she hurried over to Stephanie. She looked worried.

"What's wrong, Al?" Stephanie asked. "This is going great."

"It's not the taped segments I'm nervous about," Allie told her. "It's everything else. We still have to put the basic set together for our anchors. There's touch-up painting and lighting to figure out. It's all stuff nobody wants to do because it's boring grunt work. And we're supposed to go on the air Monday!"

"It's all right," Stephanie said. She went over a checklist for the shoot while she talked. "It will all get done. Just relax."

Stephanie glanced around. Shawna, the reporter, still wasn't in place. "Shawna!" she bellowed. Shawna came running over, fluffing her hair and straightening her outfit.

"Sorry!" she called.

"Start out by the jewelry counter, and then walk over to the stuffed animals," Stephanie ordered. "I think it will work better if we get some movement into this!"

"*I* don't," Josh argued. "I already have this shot set up. And *I'm* the director."

"Steph," Allie begged. "Let Josh handle this. Listen to me. We're really behind."

Stephanie tried to listen, but her eyes kept wandering over to what Josh and Shawna were doing.

"Shawna, you should hold the earrings up to your ears!" she yelled. "But don't put them on. We'd have to buy them!"

Stephanie turned to Allie. "Don't go anywhere. I'll be right back." She rushed over to the earring counter to choose the right pair of earrings for Shawna. She moved the reporter over to the jewelry counter. Then she turned to Josh. "Listen, having her start out here is going to work. Trust me."

"Ahem. Stephanie, could I talk to you for a minute?"

Stephanie turned to see Ms. Blith standing by the poster rack. Reluctantly, Stephanie headed over to talk. Every minute spent in discussion was one less minute to figure out the shoot.

"It looks like things are in order here, Stephanie," the teacher said. "But I've been running through the tape we have already. I think we're going to need more filler. We don't have enough material for the first newscast."

"How can that be?" Stephanie asked. "We've shot so much!"

"They're only two- and three-minute spots," the teacher reminded her.

Out of the corner of her eye Stephanie saw Josh positioning Shawna so that she faced the cash register. That wasn't right.

"Josh, she should face the stuffed animals!" Stephanie hollered across the store.

"Stephanie, did you hear what I said?" Ms. Blith asked.

"We'll just stretch some things," Stephanie assured her.

She began flipping through the posters. Which poster should face out for the shoot? The picture of a tractor being lifted by a huge tornado or the one of her favorite band?

"Stephanie," the teacher warned. "This is important."

"Ms. Blith, everything will be fine," Stephanie assured her. "I'm the producer, and I should know. I've seen my dad handle this kind of thing dozens of times on his show."

Ms. Blith studied Stephanie's face. "Well, if you're sure things are under control . . ."

"They are, Ms. Blith." Stephanie showed her the shooting schedule, prop checklist, and all her notes for the Hot Spot.

"You *are* very organized for these shoots," Ms. Blith finally said. "But you've got to learn to listen to other people's concerns."

"I am listening," Stephanie called, turning away. "Hey—Gia? How's that wavy screen coming along?"

"Check this out!" Gia said excitedly.

Stephanie hurried over and peered at the camcorder view screen. The picture of Shawna blurred and went all ripply.

"This effect is incredible," Stephanie told Gia.

"Yeah! I'm glad you thought of using it." Gia smiled.

Stephanie felt a familiar pang of conscience. She was still taking credit for Maura's ideas. The more she thought about it, the more Stephanie knew she was being completely dishonest.

That's it, Stephanie decided. I'm going to stop avoiding Maura in front of everyone. And I'll tell the class where those ideas really came from.

There! The guilty feelings disappeared.

I'm going to tell my friends the truth, Stephanie promised herself. *No matter what.*

After school the next day Stephanie made plans with Darcy and Allie to go to the mall to shop and have fun. D.J. was going to drop Michelle off there for a haircut later. Stephanie figured it would be a good place to talk.

This is it, she told herself as they got on the bus after school. I'm going to tell them all about Maura—about the video ideas and how we're friends again. They'll understand. I know they will.

All during the bus ride to the mall, Stephanie waited for a chance to begin. She kept quiet, hoping for a break in the conversation. But Darcy and Allie were discussing a movie they had seen the weekend before. And they just kept talking.

"Too bad you had to do all that stuff with Michelle, Steph," Darcy was saying. "*Thunderbolt 2* was awesome."

"I haven't seen anything like it since *Thunderbolt 1*," Allie agreed. "I'll see it again if you want to, Steph."

"Me, too," Darcy said quickly. "It's more fun to do stuff when it's the three of us together."

It's now or never, Steph thought. I might as well tell them right now.

"Listen, you guys," she said. "There's something you need to know about the video project."

"You finally assigned setup tasks?" Allie guessed. "How did you ever get people to agree to build sets this weekend?"

"She's a genius at delegating," Darcy joked.

"Whatever," Allie said. "As long as everything will be ready by Monday."

Stephanie groaned. She'd totally forgotten about the sets. They didn't have much time left. There was only the weekend. And then showtime!

She couldn't admit that to Allie and Darcy. Telling them about Maura was going to be hard enough. She couldn't admit that she was falling behind with the newscast, too.

"I told you not to worry," Stephanie said, trying to sound calm.

The bus came to a stop at the mall, and the conversation was dropped as they made their way inside.

Riding the escalator, Stephanie tried once again to gear herself up for the big talk. But now she was in a lousy mood. She felt upset about the show. She needed to feel sure of herself. Confident. And she didn't feel that way at all.

She followed her friends inside The Funky Trunk, a clothing store. Idly, she flipped through a rack of clothes. Finally she drew out a black velvet top.

"This is kind of cool," she told Darcy and Allie. "You know what? I can see Maura wearing it!"

"Maura Potter?" Darcy said, surprised. "What made you think of her?"

"Oh, I don't know," Stephanie answered as they wandered back into the mall. "I guess I've been thinking about her a lot lately."

"Stephanie!" a familiar voice suddenly rang out. Stephanie glanced down the hall.

It was Maura! She was carrying a bag from that music store everyone made fun of, The Classical Music Man.

"Stephanie!" Maura called again. She held up the shopping bag. "You have to see what I just got."

"That's a coincidence," Allie commented. "You were just talking about her. And here she is."

"Yeah," Darcy added, sounding surprised. "And she wants to talk to you, Steph."

"Listen," Stephanie began. "You know all those cool ideas—"

Stephanie stopped talking as she heard a laugh behind her. Stephanie turned. A whole group of girls from John Muir were coming up behind her. Gia and Shawna were with them.

Stephanie couldn't believe this was happening. This was exactly when she should go up to Maura. Tell her how glad she was to see her, and then tell her best friends the whole truth.

She didn't want an audience when she did it! If Stephanie even nodded at Maura in front of other people from school, chances were her social life would be over in two seconds flat.

Maura had a smile on her face as she neared Stephanie. She's excited to see me, Stephanie thought miserably.

She peered over her shoulder. The other girls from school noticed Stephanie, Darcy, and Allie, too. Now *they* were coming over to say hi!

"They had a great new selection of jazz," Maura explained as she came up to Stephanie. "Maybe we could listen to these CDs together."

Stephanie didn't know what to do, so she did the only thing she could for her social survival. She turned her back on Maura. And completely ignored her.

"Stephanie?" Maura stood directly behind her. Her voice sounded confused. "Didn't you hear me calling you?"

"I'm sorry," Stephanie said in a cold tone. "Were you speaking to me?" She didn't even turn around.

111

Stephanie knew Maura was staring at her. Her gaze bored right through the back of her head.

"Oh! Hi, Gia! Hi, Shawna!" Stephanie called a little too loudly. She began walking away quickly.

Darcy and Allie walked next to her. Stephanie turned to check their expressions. They were both glaring at her as if she were crazy. "Stephanie!" Allie said through clenched teeth. "What is going on here?"

"I'll explain later," Stephanie whispered back.

Stephanie peeked over her shoulder at Maura. The girl stood frozen to her spot. Her shoulders drooped, and she wore a hurt, bewildered expression. Stephanie thought she noticed tears welling up in Maura's eyes.

Finally she turned and began to walk away.

A wave of nausea hit Stephanie all at once. What had she done?

I can't believe I just completely ignored Maura! she thought. I am no better than the Flamingoes! How could I be that way? How could I treat a friend so badly?

Stephanie stopped in her tracks. She turned and took off for Maura.

"Wait, Maura!" she shouted. "Let me explain!"

"Stephanie! Where are you going?" Darcy called. She followed after Stephanie with Allie, Shawna, and Gia close behind.

Stephanie sped across the mall just as Maura disappeared into the crowd.

CHAPTER
14

◆ ◄ ▸ ◆

Stephanie weaved through the sea of shoppers and finally caught sight of Maura.

She reached out and grabbed her friend's arm. "Please, Maura. I need to explain . . ."

Maura whirled on Stephanie. "Explain what?" she asked in a cold, angry voice. "How you lied to me?"

Darcy, Allie, Shawna, and Gia came to a stop behind Stephanie.

"How could you do it, Stephanie?" Maura continued. "How could you lead me to believe we were friends again? I can't believe I was so stupid. I can't believe I didn't see that you were using me."

She glanced over at Darcy, Allie, Shawna, and Gia. "I bet they don't even know, do they? I bet

113

they have no idea that all your great ideas for *Scribe TV* were mine!"

Stephanie was aware of Maura's voice echoing through the mall. Everyone there could hear every word.

Maura continued without giving Stephanie a chance to talk. "Well, that's over with. From now on, Ms. Producer, you're on your own. I'm not going to give you any more ideas for your stupid video-journalism course ever again!"

Maura turned on her heel and stormed out of the mall.

Stephanie stood there a moment, her head down. She couldn't help feeling she had acted like a terrible, terrible person.

"It's true, isn't it?" Darcy said behind her. Startled, Stephanie faced her friends. She had almost forgotten they were there.

Darcy stared at Stephanie as if she were a stranger. "What Maura said—that's what you were trying to tell us just now, wasn't it?"

"I can't believe it," Gia said. "She's been giving you those great ideas all along? And you haven't said a word? You've been pretending they're yours?"

"Not only that, you used them as proof that you should be the producer!" Shawna added. "You pretended that you knew everything. You wouldn't listen to our ideas. When you didn't really know much more than we did."

"I have been trying to tell you. But it hasn't been easy," Stephanie tried to explain.

"Why didn't you trust us to give Maura a chance?" Allie asked softly. "Why did you keep so much from us?"

"Listen," Stephanie said tearfully. "I'm sorry. I—"

Darcy tugged on Allie's arm. "Come on, Al. We don't have to hang around listening to any dumb excuses."

"And we certainly don't need to stick around, either," Gia said.

"Yeah. Let's go," Shawna agreed.

Stephanie watched her friends walk away. She glanced around for the nearest bench and plopped down into it. She rested her head in her hands.

She knew the truth about Maura would soon be all over school. That didn't matter.

What *did* matter was that all her friends hated her. And they had every right to. She had acted like a complete jerk.

D.J. dropped Michelle off at the mall a few minutes later.

"Let's go," Stephanie said in a flat tone. She led her sister to the Heads-Up Salon. "Let's get this over with as soon as possible."

"Hey, what's wrong with you?" Michelle asked.

"Nothing," Stephanie answered quickly. She knew it wasn't Michelle's fault that her life was such a mess, but she didn't want to talk about it. It was too hard to pretend to be cheerful at the moment. She just felt completely awful.

If only she'd thought things out before leaping into that producer job. If only she'd been honest with Maura . . .

"Look at this!" Michelle pointed to a sign in the salon window. " 'Special on perms today! Only twenty-five dollars!' " She turned to Stephanie. "That would be *sooo* cool? Can I get one? Please?"

"Huh?" Stephanie mumbled. "No, Michelle. No way."

"Why not?" Michelle asked. "It would be so great!"

"You know Dad would flip if you got a perm. Sorry, but you just can't—" Stephanie stopped short. She peered through the crowd. Was that Maura at the other end of the hall? Walking to the newsstand?

She could catch up with her. Apologize.

"Here!" Stephanie shoved the money for the haircut at Michelle. "Take this and go inside. I've got to do something."

In a flash, Stephanie took off. She raced for the newsstand. No one was there. But a little farther down, Stephanie spotted a girl with long, dark hair. Maura! She bolted down the corridor. Stephanie turned a corner, but Maura was gone.

Stephanie was determined to find her. I'll check every store in the mall if I have to, she told herself.

She went into bookstores, department stores, clothing stores, even a store that sold golf accessories—though it was kind of hard to imagine Maura playing golf.

Maura seemed to have vanished.

Stephanie gave up the search when she caught sight of a big clock in the center of the mall. Forty minutes had passed. I'd better check on Michelle, she realized. She hurried back to the hair salon.

Michelle was standing by the register, happily paying for her haircut—and her perm.

Her *perm?* Stephanie stared at Michelle's head. Her straight blond hair was now a mass of tight corkscrew curls.

"Oh, Michelle!" Stephanie groaned.

"Hey, Steph," Michelle said. "What do you think?"

Stephanie was too upset for more lies. "I think it's terrible!" she said. "Why did you do it?"

"You left. I figured you didn't care how they did my hair. And besides"—Michelle fluffed her curls with her hand—"I think it looks cool!"

Stephanie grabbed Michelle's hand. "We're going home. Now!"

How am I going to fix this? Stephanie wondered on the bus ride back. How am I going to get this silly perm out of Michelle's hair before Dad comes home from his shoot tomorrow?

Twenty minutes later she dragged Michelle off

the bus and up the steps to their house. The sooner they got inside, the sooner she could begin work.

Michelle squirmed as they reached the front door. "Why are you acting like such a nut?"

"Just come with me!" Stephanie ordered. She opened the front door and froze as Becky's voice floated toward her from the kitchen.

"So, honey, how was it taking care of the twins without me?" she asked Jesse.

Stephanie couldn't believe it. Becky was home early from the location shoot! And that meant . . .

"Yeah, how did it go?" Danny asked.

Dad's home, too! Stephanie thought desperately. What else could possibly go wrong?

She forced herself to think rationally. She had to sneak Michelle upstairs. Maybe she could wash Michelle's hair twenty times in a row to straighten it a bit. Or set it on really large rollers. Anything was worth a try!

"Shhh!" she hissed to Michelle as she tugged her up the steps. "Be quiet now. We don't want Dad to hear us."

"Why not?" Michelle asked loudly.

"Steph? Michelle, honey?" Danny called out. "Is that you?"

Oh, no, Stephanie thought. They were caught!

CHAPTER
15

◆ ◢ ◆ ◆

"Hey, Michelle! I—" Danny stopped midsentence. "Oh, no. What happened to your hair?" Danny spun Michelle around in the living room. He checked her hair from all angles. "It's . . . unbelievable!"

"Unbelievable good?" Stephanie asked hopefully.

"Unbelievable bad!" Danny yelled. "Michelle, you're way too young to be getting perms!"

"It's okay, Dad," Michelle said quickly. "It's not a *real* perm. I only got it curled. I can wash it out right away."

"*What?*" Stephanie glared at her. "Why didn't you tell me? I thought you got a perm."

Michelle grinned. "It was a joke, Steph. A funny, *hair-raising* joke. Don't you think it's hysterical?"

"No!" Stephanie shouted.

"Steph, honey. I was waiting for you to get home," Danny said. "We need to talk."

Danny led Stephanie into the kitchen and sat her down in a chair. He had a disapproving look on his face. Stephanie gazed at the floor, ready for a lecture.

"I know you were surprised about Michelle's hair," she said quickly. "But everything's fine now. It will be back to normal by tomorrow."

"That's true," Danny told her. "But obviously, you weren't paying attention to what Michelle was doing."

"I'm really sorry about the hair," Stephanie told him.

"Well, that isn't a major catastrophe," Danny said slowly. "But it's not just the hair, honey."

He held out the mail. "I got this huge bill from the credit card company. What did you buy at The Sporting Life that cost so much money? And then there's this new credit card I received. What happened to the old one?"

"I—" Steph started to say, but Danny cut her off.

"You lost it." Danny answered his question before Stephanie could. "And apparently you weren't very attentive to Michelle at the sporting goods store, either." He sighed. "It seems that wherever you and Michelle went while I was away, trouble followed. And left a huge mess."

Stephanie felt as though a huge cotton ball were

stuck in her throat. She tried to swallow, but it didn't work. She could barely talk.

"It's all my fault," she admitted softly. "I haven't really been watching Michelle, making sure things get done."

"I'm going to ask D.J. to finish helping Michelle," Danny told her. "She's free starting next week. And, honey, I have to tell you, I don't feel you're ready for your own credit card yet. I'm sorry. But I have to stick by my original decision. You're just too young."

"I understand," Stephanie said in a small voice. "May I be excused?"

Danny nodded and Stephanie trudged upstairs. She fought to hold back the tears until she got to her room. But she didn't succeed.

Crying hard, she flung herself on the bed. She felt terrible. Not because her father refused to give her a credit card. She could live with that. It was just that now *everything* in her world was going down the drain.

Danny was disappointed in her and thought she was immature. And he was right. Stephanie realized she'd been helping Michelle only because she'd wanted that credit card. That was nothing to be proud of.

Then there was the disaster with Darcy and Allie. Her best friends were furious with her. Gia and Shawna were pretty mad, too. And so was Maura. Maura would probably never speak to her again for pretending they were friends. Or was it for pretending they weren't friends? Either way, Stephanie felt lousy.

The worst part of all was that Stephanie knew they were right. She'd been awful.

The doorbell rang, and Stephanie sat up in bed. She waited for someone to answer it, but no one did. Wiping her eyes, she trudged downstairs.

Stephanie peered through the window at Sue Kramer and Bill Klepper. She felt a little better. *At least there are two people who aren't mad at me*, she thought.

"Hi," she said, opening the door. "Come on in!"

Neither Bill nor Sue looked at Stephanie. Instead, Bill spoke to a spot above his head. "No, thank you," he said in a stiff, polite voice. "We'd rather stay right here."

"We have something to say," Sue told Stephanie. "And then we'll leave."

Uh-oh, Stephanie thought. This doesn't sound good.

"We heard about your little scam with Maura Potter," Sue continued. "And we're all really angry."

"What do you mean *all*? You mean the whole class?" Stephanie's heart sank. Now everyone on the video project hated her, too.

"We organized a telephone poll this afternoon," Sue told her. "And we took a vote. You're not producer anymore.

"You're fired!"

CHAPTER
16

◆ ◀ ◗ ◆

Saturday night Stephanie lay on her bed and stared up at the ceiling. So many things in her life were going wrong.

How have I screwed things up? Stephanie mused to herself. Let me count the ways. First, she let down her dad, who was counting on her help. Second, she lied to the staff on *Scribe TV*, whom she was supposed to lead. Third, she hurt someone who didn't deserve it. Someone who was a very good friend.

I have to do something, Stephanie realized. I can't mope around for the rest of my life, blaming myself for these problems. Sure, I created them. So what that means is, I've got to do my best to fix them!

But how? Stephanie wondered. She thought far

into the night, until finally she came up with a plan. A three-pronged plan that would make everything okay again.

Sunlight streamed through the window. It was Sunday morning, but Stephanie had set her alarm for her weekday wake-up time, 7:15. She would have to get an early start if she expected to accomplish everything in her plan.

Across the room, Michelle rolled over with an annoyed grunt.

Stephanie lowered the volume on her radio and listened for the first song of the day. She smiled as she heard "Take Some Action." Perfect! She planned to do just that. She was going to try to make things right.

For phase one of the plan, Stephanie went down to breakfast. She knew her dad would be up early. She explained that she really did want to help him, and that she could still do that if he drove her to the mall that morning.

Fortunately, her dad agreed. Two hours later Stephanie stood at the entrance to the mall. She waited for the doors to open. Then she rushed inside.

Stephanie took a carefully written list that she had made the night before out of her pocket. She read from the first part. "Let's see," she said. "Sneaker Corner, then Kidz Storz for T-shirts, and then Write On for stationery and such."

She whizzed all around the mall, darting into store after store. She spent the rest of the morning and the early afternoon shopping. It was a marathon spree, getting every single one of the rest of Michelle's camp things.

Stephanie was grateful that her father had agreed to trust her with his credit card one more time. She even threw in a special surprise for Michelle using her own money: a pair of glow-in-the-dark flip-flops.

Danny picked Stephanie up at the mall. Whew! she thought after she dropped off the shopping bags. Now I'm ready for phase two of my plan—show the staff of *Scribe TV* that I really am committed to the show.

Stephanie scarfed down a quick peanut butter sandwich for lunch. Then she grabbed her bike and set out for John Muir.

At school she rang the bell on the side of the building. "Please, Mr. Jasper," she said to the custodian when he opened the door. "I need to get to the *Scribe TV* set in the cafeteria."

Nodding, he let her in. *Now*, Stephanie thought, *I have to get the set ready!*

All that afternoon Stephanie hammered, nailed, and put the finishing touches on the backdrop: a mural of John Muir.

She stood back to admire her work. *Hmmm*, she thought. *It could use a little something extra.* Stephanie glanced around the set. Someone had brought in a string of Christmas lights.

That's it! Stephanie thought. She arranged the lights behind the canvas mural so that it looked like there were lights in all the windows of the classrooms.

"Let's see," she said out loud. She sat back on her heels to rest. "What else does *Scribe TV* need? Something that no one has thought to do."

Stephanie snapped her fingers. The extra time they needed to fill on air. Maybe she could do something about that. But what?

She didn't have a clue. She certainly couldn't ask Maura this time. She decided to make a list of ideas. Seconds later she grimaced and tossed the list in the garbage.

Then it hit her. She knew exactly what to do with the time. If she did it right, it would take care of phase three of her plan.

I hope it works. Stephanie crossed her fingers.

No, she thought. I can't just hope. It has to work. It just has to!

CHAPTER
17

◆ ◀ ◼ ◆

Early Monday morning the staff of *Scribe TV* was scheduled to gather at the set in the cafeteria. This would be their last meeting before the show went on-air to every homeroom in the school!

Stephanie stood at the front of the room, waiting for everyone to arrive. She tried not to look as scared as she felt. Her stomach was doing somersaults. This was not going to be easy.

"What's she doing here?" Tiffany asked as she entered the room. "I thought we fired her."

Shawna, Josh, Gia, Darcy, Allie, and the entire staff of *Scribe TV* filed in after her. Ms. Blith brought up the rear.

"I'm here to apologize to you all," Stephanie announced. "I should never have let everyone think that Maura's ideas were mine. And I should have listened to other people. You all had a lot to contribute. I was really a pigheaded know-it-all. I'm sorry."

"Talk's cheap, Stephanie," Josh said. "We were all pretty hurt by what you did."

The rest of the staff voiced their agreement.

"Hey, wait," Allie interrupted. "The set is finished! Everything's done!"

Stephanie held her breath as everyone turned to the set. Would they like what she had done?

"But, I don't understand. It was only half-finished when we left on Friday," Gia stated.

"Yeah, and it looked pretty sad," Josh agreed. "But look at it now!"

"Check out the lights in the backdrop!" Shawna exclaimed. "They're totally cool."

"All right," Ms. Blith spoke up. "'Fess up. Who did all this work while I wasn't looking!"

"I did," Steph told them.

The staff looked at her, dumbfounded.

"I came in on Sunday and finished it all," she stated. "I just wanted to show you how much I'm really committed to *Scribe TV*. Even if I screwed up royally before."

"Wow, Steph," Allie said. "You must have been here all day."

Stephanie shrugged.

"Thanks," Allie said, smiling. "This was really great!"

"Yeah," Darcy added warmly. "You really did the right thing here."

Stephanie smiled at her friends. They didn't sound so mad anymore. Two down, the rest of the class to go.

"So—will you let me back on the staff?" Stephanie asked sheepishly. "Please?"

Later that morning in the media arts room, Stephanie watched the monitor on the control board.

"This is Darcy Powell, reporting for *Scribe TV*. Back to you, Sue and Bill!" Darcy said on the screen.

"Cut to live feed—now!" Stephanie told Josh. He pressed a button on the board. Darcy switched off, and Bill and Sue appeared on the screen. They sat at the *Scribe TV* set, reading from Allie's script. They were about to wrap up the first show. Hopefully, it wouldn't be the last.

Stephanie sighed with relief. Not only had the staff let her back on the project, they reinstated her as producer. The show went amazingly well.

The live coverage worked out great. The anchors read smoothly, and the show moved along at a quick pace.

At the top right-hand corner of the screen, a different image of a scribe blipped on every thirty seconds. It looked terrific.

Everything, in fact, looked terrific. There was just one more thing the show needed. . . .

Stephanie hurried over to Ms. Blith. She'd already told the teacher—but no one else—her idea to end the newscast. It was almost time to put her plan into action.

"Go over to the set," Ms. Blith said. "I'll man the control board with Josh."

"Thanks." Stephanie strode from the media room over to the cafeteria. She approached the *Scribe TV* set and sat in the big armchair next to the couch.

"And now our producer, Stephanie Tanner," Sue said.

Gia swung the camera around so that it pointed directly at Stephanie. Her heart pounded as she looked into the black eye of the lens. Suddenly she felt so nervous, but she forced herself to take a deep breath.

"A *Scribe TV* editorial," Stephanie said calmly. She glanced down at the notes she had made for her appearance.

"It is time for everyone at John Muir to become a little more tolerant of one another," she began. She took another breath. She'd never meant anything so much in her life.

"We have all kinds of students here. People of many different races and different religions.

"Somehow, we all know to keep an open mind about *those* differences. But the students of John

Muir discriminate against each other in a different way. But one that is just as hurtful and insensitive.

"There are people here, not only of different races, but with different *ideas*. Different *styles*. People who don't fit the norm.

"For some reason, these people are usually branded un-popular, nerdy, or un-cool. And other people are afraid to be friends with them because of that. Well, in my opinion, that's just plain wrong," Stephanie asserted.

"We need to understand and accept *all* our differences. We need to welcome them, in fact, because that's how we grow and learn. And because the differences among us are what make things interesting." She paused for a moment.

"And now, everyone at *Scribe TV* would like to thank *Maura Potter* for all her help with this broadcast. All the funky, fun things you've seen today were Maura's ideas. And it was her vision that has helped to make this show possible. Thanks, Maura.

"And personally, *I'd* like to thank Maura for being there whenever I needed her. And for becoming a close friend these past weeks. I hope that we can continue to be friends for a long time." She paused a moment.

"This is Stephanie Tanner signing off," she finished.

Gia swung the camera back around to Bill and Sue.

"Well, that's our first show," Sue wrapped up.

"Join us again," Bill added. "Same time, same place!"

The *Scribe TV* theme music blared over the speakers on the set. The red light on top of the camera blinked off. The show was over!

A cheer went up from everyone on the set. Stephanie sunk back into the armchair. Whew! What a relief. The show was a hit. And she had accomplished phase three of her plan. The question was—had it worked?

Would Maura actually forgive her?

CHAPTER
18

◆ ◀ ◢ ◆

People approached Stephanie about her editorial all day. Most of them agreed with what she had to say, and everyone told her they admired her courage in saying what she felt.

Stephanie accepted the praise—and the criticism—graciously. But there was one person who had not approached her. The one person she truly wanted to see. Maura.

When the last bell rang, Stephanie had not so much as caught a glimpse of her.

She left her last class and trudged to her locker. She spun her combination.

"Hey, Steph." Allie tapped her on the shoulder. Darcy stood next to her.

"No one can stop talking about *Scribe TV!*" Allie

said, excited. "Looks like we'll definitely be on in the fall!"

"Great," Stephanie muttered.

"You could try to sound a *little* happier about it," Darcy pointed out.

"Sorry." Stephanie turned back to her locker to pack her books. "It's kind of hard to be enthusiastic when Maura hasn't even tried to talk to me."

She sighed. "Oh, well. I tried my best to apologize. I guess it just wasn't good enough."

Allie gave Stephanie a quick squeeze. "I thought you did a great job."

"Me, too," Darcy agreed.

"Umm—I did, too," a third voice said.

Stephanie whirled around. Maura stood in front of her, smiling.

"I thought a lot about what you said on TV this morning. Is that how you really feel, Steph?" she asked.

"Absolutely," Stephanie insisted. "I wouldn't have broadcast it to the whole school if I didn't. But let me add something I didn't say on TV—I was stupid, Maura. And mean. And I am so sorry. I really do think of you as my friend. I hope you'll give me another chance."

Maura giggled. "How could I not give you a chance with an apology like that?"

"You couldn't!" Darcy said, putting an arm around Stephanie.

"How about we all hang out after school today?" Allie suggested.

Maura gazed down at the floor.

"*All* of us," Allie added for emphasis.

Maura looked up with a happy expression.

Stephanie laughed. "Great! I know just the thing to do."

"What's that?" Darcy asked.

"You can all help me sew a thousand tags into Michelle's camp clothes!"

"Ugh!" Darcy groaned.

"No way!" Allie protested.

"I think I've helped you enough for the rest of my life," Maura added. "You owe me, Tanner. Big-time!"

"Fine," Steph agreed, "how about I buy you all cookies at the marina?"

"Sounds great!" Maura said.

The three girls left the school building together and walked over to the bus stop.

"Hey, Maura. Think we can go to that booth with the secondhand clothes?" Darcy asked. "I think I'd like to pick up a really funky vest to wear over my new jeans."

"Sure," Maura said. "I know where the owner of the booth keeps all her best stuff."

Stephanie observed her three friends, all getting along.

She smiled, and thought an appropriate song to wake up to tomorrow would be "Happy Days Are Here Again!"

FULL HOUSE™
Club Stephanie

*S*tephanie and her friends are looking forward to a summer full of sailing fun! There's just one problem: the super-rotten, super-snooty group called the Flamingoes....

Too Many Flamingoes
(Coming mid-May 1998)

Friend or Flamingo?
(Coming mid-June 1998)

Flamingoes Overboard!
(Coming mid-July 1998)

Collect all three books in this brand-new trilogy!

Based on the hit Warner Bros. TV series

A MINSTREL® BOOK

Published by Pocket Books

1357-02

FULL HOUSE™
Michelle

#5: THE GHOST IN MY CLOSET 53573-0/$3.99

#6: BALLET SURPRISE 53574-9/$3.99

#7: MAJOR LEAGUE TROUBLE 53575-7/$3.99

#8: MY FOURTH-GRADE MESS 53576-5/$3.99

#9: BUNK 3, TEDDY, AND ME 56834-5/$3.99

#10: MY BEST FRIEND IS A MOVIE STAR!
(Super Edition) 56835-3/$3.99

#11: THE BIG TURKEY ESCAPE 56836-1/$3.99

#12: THE SUBSTITUTE TEACHER 00364-X/$3.99

#13: CALLING ALL PLANETS 00365-8/$3.99

#14: I'VE GOT A SECRET 00366-6/$3.99

#15: HOW TO BE COOL 00833-1/$3.99

#16: THE NOT-SO-GREAT OUTDOORS 00835-8/$3.99

#17: MY HO-HO-HORRIBLE CHRISTMAS 00836-6/$3.99

MY AWESOME HOLIDAY FRIENDSHIP BOOK
(An Activity Book) 00840-4/$3.99

FULL HOUSE MICHELLE OMNIBUS 02181-8/$6.99

#18: MY ALMOST PERFECT PLAN 00837-4/$3.99

#19: APRIL FOOLS 01729-2/$3.99

4.97

A MINSTREL® BOOK
Published by Pocket Books

Simon & Schuster Mail Order Dept. BWB
200 Old Tappan Rd., Old Tappan, N.J. 07675

Please send me the books I have checked above. I am enclosing $ 5.00 (please add $0.75 to cover the

postage and handling for each order. Please add appropriate sales tax). Send check or money order--no cash or C.O.D.'s please. Allow up to

six weeks for delivery. For purchase over $10.00 you may use VISA: card number, expiration date and customer signature must be included.

Name ___I_____

Address __8035 E Beddows Ct._____

City __Fort Meade_____ State/Zip _MD 80755__

VISA Card # _____ Exp.Date _____

Signature _____

1033-26

FULL HOUSE Stephanie™

PHONE CALL FROM A FLAMINGO	88004-7/$3.99
THE BOY-OH-BOY NEXT DOOR	88121-3/$3.99
TWIN TROUBLES	88290-2/$3.99
HIP HOP TILL YOU DROP	88291-0/$3.99
HERE COMES THE BRAND NEW ME	89858-2/$3.99
THE SECRET'S OUT	89859-0/$3.99
DADDY'S NOT-SO-LITTLE GIRL	89860-4/$3.99
P.S. FRIENDS FOREVER	89861-2/$3.99
GETTING EVEN WITH THE FLAMINGOES	52273-6/$3.99
THE DUDE OF MY DREAMS	52274-4/$3.99
BACK-TO-SCHOOL COOL	52275-2/$3.99
PICTURE ME FAMOUS	52276-0/$3.99
TWO-FOR-ONE CHRISTMAS FUN	53546-3/$3.99
THE BIG FIX-UP MIX-UP	53547-1/$3.99
TEN WAYS TO WRECK A DATE	53548-X/$3.99
WISH UPON A VCR	53549-8/$3.99
DOUBLES OR NOTHING	56841-8/$3.99
SUGAR AND SPICE ADVICE	56842-6/$3.99
NEVER TRUST A FLAMINGO	56843-4/$3.99
THE TRUTH ABOUT BOYS	00361-5/$3.99
CRAZY ABOUT THE FUTURE	00362-3/$3.99
MY SECRET ADMIRER	00363-1/$3.99
BLUE RIBBON CHRISTMAS	00830-7/$3.99
THE STORY ON OLDER BOYS	00831-5/$3.99
MY THREE WEEKS AS A SPY	00832-3/$3.99

Available from Minstrel® Books Published by Pocket Books